Single and alone, Eve Windsong finds her long-lost father and his family at the Sugarland Lodge in the Great Smoky Mountain National Park. When her father's family needs help, Eve jumps in, hoping to finally belong somewhere.

Sunny Days, her new sister, believes love is the only family Eve needs. To get Sunny off her back, Eve agrees to try MountainMatch.com. When a handsome hunk announces he's arrived to hook her up, she mistakes his job as the cable guy for an online date.

When she overcomes her faulty assumption, the global pandemic reaches the mountains. A quarantine is issued and the National Guard commandeers the Lodge. Eve and Beau are forced to live together for who knows how long. Just as they begin to adjust to their Covid-habitation along with Beau's ex-wife and his tattooed teenage son, Eve learns his ex wants to rebuild their fractured family.

Can Eve and Beau's connection last beyond the pandemic, or will it remain a temporary hookup?

Mountain Hookup
Copyright © 2021 Kathy Kalmar
ISBN: 978-1-4874-3007-8
Cover art by Martine Jardin

Published by eXtasy Books Inc or
Devine Destinies, an imprint of eXtasy Books Inc

Look for us online at:
www.eXtasybooks.com or www.devinedestinies.com

Mountain Hookup
Mountain Series 13

By

Kathy Kalmar

DEDICATION

To Larry who gave me my very own second chance to love, more happiness than I could have believed possible and healed three broken hearts in the process, you are my true love.
And
As promised, to my best friend, Ron Wilson

In Memoriam

To my forever friend, Linda Wilson, whose skills, talents, and belief in me and my work led to this publication. Ours is a relationship forged in the fires of pain, loss, love and laughter. How I wish you could have seen this work.

Acknowledgment

For Carolyn Gilbreath, her counsel and encouragement made this a better book. She is my Best Friend Forever and Beta reader extraordinaire. For Cheri Zisler for her online dating lore, help and friendship. And to Doug Marple, webmaster, who keeps the social media site wheels turning. I'm grateful to you all.
And with great gratitude, I acknowledge Jay Austin, extraordinary Editor in Chief; Debbie Nygaard, editor; Martine Jardin, artist; Bri Vries, Assistant to Editor in Chief; The Greater Detroit Romance Writers of America; and you, my readers.

CHAPTER ONE: ONLY THE GOOD DIE YOUNG

"Eve Windsong?" asked a tall, dark, and handsome man with silver hair at his temples. He looked fit and wore dark blue well-filled tight pants, a blue baseball cap, and a light blue dress shirt open at the collar that revealed a hint of dark tufts of hair.

Eve nodded. "Yes. How can I help you?"

A glint appeared within the depths of his dark slate eyes as his gaze traveled up and down the length of her. "You ready to hookup?" He strode forward, heading to room one. "All set for me? I like to get things in order before I begin. Mind if I go in first?"

Eve's face flooded with heat, and she raised an eyebrow. She choked out a response, trying to dismiss unbidden hot images of riding crops, silken ropes, and blindfolds. *What the hell am I thinking?* "Excuse me?"

"Hold on a second. Damned if you don't look like one of the Weathers Girls."

"Yeah, I get that a lot."

He looked at her questioningly.

"Long story," she muttered.

The silver fox whipped out his phone, swiped left a few times, found what he was after, and asked, "This Route Two? Gatlinburg? Sugarlands Lodge?"

Eve nodded.

"Eve?"

1

In a no-nonsense tone, she said, "We've already established that."

A cocky grin crossed his firm, kissable lips. "I believe you are expecting me?"

Surprise shot through her body. "Hardly."

He looked up confidently. "You said Eve Windsong, right? Our hookup date is today."

"I don't know what planet you're from, but I most certainly did not request a hookup."

He checked his tablet again. "I'm your man, and we have a date—"

"Really? Do you have any idea how often I've heard that line the past several weeks?" She swallowed her disdain. *God help me, I pray I didn't just pant. I feel like a bitch in heat. I hope I don't look as hot to trot as I feel right now.*

He looked at her with the question still in his gaze. "No, but I'm at your service. Ready, willing, and able. When you are, of course. Don't want to get ahead of myself or anything. I can wait. No hurry." He winked. "I just have to get a few things." He looked around as if whatever he needed had disappeared. "Oh, yeah, that's right, I remember now." He snapped his fingers. "I got this. Hang on a second. I'm a tad bit rusty at this game."

Eve straightened and took a deep breath. If it was possible, her skin flushed even deeper. *Here we go again. At least he admits this is a* game. *Better to stop this farce right in its tracks.* "Look, I'm working. It's clear I obviously need to change my profile. There's been a mistake."

It was his turn to look confused and at a loss. "Huh?" He shrugged. "Whatever. I'm new at this part of the operation. I'll be back in a jiffy. Appears I forgot my tools."

You're a tool, all right. We agree on that much. Eve sighed. *I swear I'm so gonna shoot Sunny Days on sight next time I see my half-sister's skinny little ass. At least this guy is gorgeous. But still another potential date to ditch. What the hell! No coffee? No how-*

do-you-dos? Just I'm ready *– how'd he put that? –* willing and able. *Who says that?*

As quickly as those fine fingers had snapped, she was alone. She picked up a brochure nearby and fanned herself. The man was hot. That much was certain.

A series of gawdawful encounters flashed through Eve's mind at lightning speed. Labeled as *dates,* those flashbacks had been her fate ever since Sunny posted her dating profile on MountainMatch.com.

Drat! I meant to cancel that post for good. Just been too busy learning this new job, and Sunny has been scarce lately. I haven't had the chance to review what she actually posted *on that stupid, silly dating website. Note to self – have Dawn send my laptop. How'd I even manage to forget that? And why did I ever listen to that scatterbrain Sunny, whose post has sent half a dozen losers my way?*

Eve quickly recalled some of the doozies she'd dealt with recently. A picture of a man rose in her mind's eye – at least twenty years older than the photo he had posted.

Jack Small, lifting his tie spotted with food that missed his mouth, said, "This here's my lucky tie. Every time I wear it, I get lucky. How 'bout after coffee, we get lucky at the Parkway Motel up Route 321?"

I'd barely even sat down to sip my carryout coffee when I spit it out in disbelief. My coffee joined the other stains on his lucky tie. I exited stage left, saying over my shoulder, "It's clear we're not a match."

He blasted me with hateful posts until MountainMatch.com shut down his diatribe.

Instantly, she recalled another potential date, one who'd regaled her with a litany of non-stop complaints on why all women were sluts with Daddy issues and his exes were the worst of the lot. That time she excused herself to go to the restroom and left through KT's Koffee Haus kitchen's back door. That guy actually made the aging biker dude that showed up one Friday afternoon look good in comparison.

Sunny breezed in with Hot-Stuff-On-A-Stick-Guy trailing her, now sporting a toolkit and utility belt. "What? Eve, why are you looking at me like that?"

The twinkle in Sunny's wide innocent-looking baby blues told Eve her hunches were right. Sunny might have something to do with this.

"I see you've met Beau." Looking innocent, Sunny smiled. "Beau Jobs of Garter Bytes Communications Services is here to inspect our telecommunications system. He'll start in Banquet Room One to update and rescan our communications system and the flat-screen televisions. We're going high tech here in the main building—just a little bit—to stay competitive. However, there'll still be no wireless or cable connections anywhere else. We're maintaining the rustic *getaway* vibe while the office is linked with the outside. Beau's our cable guy."

Eve looked at them. "Cable guy? Whatever you say." *He shore don't look like no cable guy I've ever seen.* Eve's own brand of Southern speak came through in her thoughts sometimes. She and her twin sister, Dawn, had been raised on a commune in the brown rolling hills of rural California.

Beau bounced on the balls of his feet as if he knew she had misunderstood him.

Is that a smirk on his face? Eve glared at him with icy politeness and nodded. "I believe you meant to say *Banquet* Room One, and certainly, be my…er…guest…er… Have at it."

Beau made a small salute. "Ma'am. If you'll excuse me, I'll get started." He gestured to the set of doors with the number one over it. "I'd like to hear more about that profile you've been talking about, but now's not the time." The man had the audacity to wink at her. Then he tossed out this idea. "But if you're talking about a *real* hookup, you've got the wrong man. I'm done lookin' in all the wrong places. I'd think you'd be, too. It's twenty years into a new century. All a woman has to do is ask. Take the same risk we men have been running for centuries. If you've got a mind to."

Eve arched a brow. "Really?"

He looked both smug and sure of himself. "Really."

She leaned forward, her chin resting on her palms. She batted her eyelashes. "Maybe I will."

A slow smile crossed his lips. "I dare you."

"You're on."

"So, ask away."

Without missing a beat, she said, "How about Sunday?"

"Sunday it is. What time and where?"

"Eleven o'clock Mass at Saint Mary's."

His big belly laugh rang through the Lodge. He cleared his throat as he recovered. "Meet you outside the church. We'll do breakfast afterward."

She gaped with an O of surprise. *Didn't see that comin'.* But then she greeted his remark with a small smile. "Fine. You can help me at the All You Can Eat Pancake Breakfast. You cook?"

"Is the Pope Catholic? Any decent, red-blooded American male can flip flapjacks as well as burgers."

She laughed. "See you then, cable guy."

Sunny had watched the interplay between them and raised a triumphant arm pump. "Don't forget about Saturday night, Beau."

He tipped his Tennessee Smokies baseball cap in Sunny's direction, nodded, and sauntered off.

"What's that all about?" Eve asked.

Sunny tossed off a careless *Nuthin* and sashayed into the waiting arms of her husband, who was joining her for a late lunch.

CHAPTER TWO: SUNNY DAYS

Eve needed to set things straight with Sunny. *Oh, I know she means well, but this quest to get me a man has got to stop.* When there was a lull in their work, Eve pulled Sunny to the rocking chairs gracing the veranda. Most guests were eating lunch or were out and about in the Great Smoky Mountain National Park in which the Lodge sat.

"Look Sunny, I know you're trying to help me settle in here, make me feel at home and all, but this is just a temporary gig—"

Sunny broke in. "Listen to you, California Girl, all gig and such…"

Eve tapped her toe with impatience. "Look, I'm here long enough to get to know my long-lost father. And to help you out, once I learned Skye has her hands full with the…what do y'all call 'em…the Squad?"

Sunny nodded, her wavy hair bouncing with her movements. "The Quad Squad, yes. I know this is temporary, but good grief, girl," she said in a stage whisper, "you're not over the hill yet just because you're over *fifty*. You need to meet people. Someone to share your life with before—"

"Don't you dare say before I get too old! I'll have you know I've been fine these past fifty-something years, and I'll be fine for the next fifty. I don't need a man to be happy. Once my fiancé, Stu, died in the Gulf War, I decided I was done with love. It's too much heartache and loss for me. I'm fine as I am. I do as I choose. Go where I wanna go. You don't understand. A woman like me loves just one man, and he's gone. And despite what you think, fifty-one isn't old."

6

"You don't have fifty years left, ya know. Just sayin'."

Eve wanted to smack her. "You know what I mean."

Sunny looked directly into Eve's eyes. "You're just scared. Still young enough for fun. Who said anything about fiancé, love, marriage? I'm talking getting laid, woman. Dating's one thing. Grieving's another. Acting like a nun isn't healthy."

Eve glared at her. "Who said I was a nun? Don't you be callin' me no nun."

"Wellll, iffin' yer not, I know you probably ain't getting none. There's been a steady stream of eligible men coming at you ever since I posted your profile, and you haven't had any that stayed the night that I can tell." Sunny smirked. "Look, ya don't have to buy the pig for a little sausage. Just have some fun."

Eve screeched. "Sunny Days, I've put up enough with your scatterbrained shenanigans. You're just like my twin. Always pulling a fast one. I've been meaning to tell you to take down my dating profile. What in heavens name have you put up there?"

Sunny just looked at her like she'd lost her mind. "Uh, let's just say, what you wrote lacked sass, and I spiced it up a tad."

"A tad? What the hell did you write? The men who've come knocking at my site are the hounds from hell. Bald. Old. Fat. Stupid… Besides, sex can give you STDs. Who says sex is healthy?"

"Duh, Doctor Ruth, that's who." Sunny looked pleased with her ability to recall those doctors from her *scatterbrained* head.

"Never heard of her." Eve wasn't having it.

Sunny continued undaunted. "Doctors from all over say the same. Remember Doctor Masters and Doctor Johnson? They're probably more familiar to ya since you're older and all. You just have to quit swipin' on the *no-good* candidates. Be more discriminating."

Eve choked. "I've been swiping on the best of the bunch. None of them look like they're old, fat, dumb, and bald. They post pictures from twenty, thirty years ago. And let me tell you, they don't take *no* for an answer. Some trolled me. Now I've got *haters,* and I've only *dated*—if you can call getting coffee *dating*—precious few of them."

Sunny didn't look or sound convinced. "We just have to tweak your profile a bit. Okay. Settle down. I'll fix it. If…"

"There's no ifs, ands, buts, or maybes about it, sister! Fix it? Shut it down." Eve made sure her tone brooked no argument.

"Give me a chance to finish my sentence, will ya? There's this one teensy-weensy, speedy event we have got to try." Sunny pinched her fingers as she spoke. "If that doesn't work, I'll take down the post. Deal?"

Eve was running out of patience. She wanted Sunny to stop and go the hell away. "I better not regret this."

Sunny looked like she had just won the lottery. A huge smile lit her face. "Trust me. My Gram said I can nag the fur off a cat, so you might as well give up. It'll be fun."

Eve raised a brow in question and shook her head. "I've heard that before. Fun for who?"

Sunny's face lost its happiness, and she leaned in as if to reveal the secrets of the universe. "You." She smiled again. "It'll be perfect for you. Mark my words. You'll thank me later. Chillax."

Eve sighed. "Knowing you, if it ain't one thing, it's ten."

Eve was glad Sunny was taking over the afternoon shift and she could leave the tsunami of Sunny's energy. And still, Sunny was going on and on about something. Wearily, Eve shook her head and agreed to try just *one* more thing. *At least she promised speed. Give it a rest, sister. Damn, but she sure is like Dawn.*

Sunny wrapped it up. "Meet me at Baily's in town at seven o'clock, and for God's sake, wear something trendy and fun."

Chapter Three: Don't Take Your Love to Town, Eve

Since it was early in the afternoon, Eve decided to kick off her sandals and leave them on the bank to pick her way across the stream. Huge boulders known as greybacks, left behind by the glaciers that formed the mountain, lay strewn like toys a child had left behind. The rocks made a careful series of steps, almost a bridge over the water. She picked her way rock by rock until she reached a boulder that was more or less secluded.

The sunlight stole through the leaves of the surrounding forest of evergreens and hardwoods, providing just the perfect blend of sun and shade to protect her fair skin. She was careful not to get too much sun. She burned easily. She lay on her back on the boulder, making a pillow with her forearms, and spread her feet and legs out on the stone.

While she looked around, savoring the deep green of the area, the brown hills of California came to mind. While beautiful in their own right, these green mountains brought her a sense of serenity and deep peace. She loved the contrast the sun made as it splayed between the leaves. The busy stream as it rushed down the hillside calmed her oddly as it raced and fell over the rocky riverbed. Other places along the stream excited her as it made its way through the hills. But now she needed peace and quiet after dealing with Sunny's energy.

Perhaps the drain she felt was really in response to the

flood of feeling Beau had caused to race through her blood. Her pulse quickened just thinking about the firm body that seemed to catch her attention despite her claims of not needing a man.

She replayed the scene of meeting Beau Jobs. He was a knockout in the looks department, but did she really *not* want a man? Or not someone as tempting as Beau? Despite those questions, she had made a promise to meet Sunny this evening, and she'd keep it.

She began mentally flipping through her wardrobe, wondering if her new vertical striped jumpsuit counted as trendy enough. Or should she wear a crisp white tailored shirt folded to her elbow and straight, tight black jeans? Oh well, she had until seven o'clock to figure that out. In the meantime, the mellow setting and gently flowing water lulled her to sleep.

She awoke refreshed and hurried back to Little Miss Muffet's cabin, where she was staying on the Lodge's premises, to prepare for the evening. The cabins complimented the rooms and suites available at the Lodge and were named after nursery rhymes. Some were larger than others and included kitchenettes. Others catered to families.

While she'd been offered quarters in the family's rooms of the Lodge's main house, she chose to assimilate much more slowly into her newly discovered family by staying in a cabin instead. That way she could keep her distance and decide how much or how little family time she wanted.

She sure had an interesting family now. The entirety of her life had been lived without the man who fathered her. Her parents connected and conceived her and her twin at Woodstock in 1969. Who knew she'd have a later-in-life need to find her roots? Her need for deeper roots had led her from California to the Sugarlands Lodge in Tennessee and to John Weathers, her birth father, and her reason for being here now. She didn't need another man to distract her. Her life was complicated enough as it was. Yet here she was, getting ready to go out on the town with her half-sister, Sunny.

She gathered her shower caddy and treated herself to a waterfall experience at the Lodge's Spa Haus. She used the touch screen to activate the multi-shower jets and selected an Enya playlist. Soft purple chromo therapy lights provided a wonderful ambiance.

Eve relaxed as the warm lilac-scented water flowed over her body. She found herself entertaining hot daydreams of silken ropes tied gently to her arms as Beau's hands slid over her like the flow of the water. She tipped her hardening nipples to the shower's gentle onslaught and pretended it was his tongue seeking to pleasure them. She turned, pretending the stream of water was the sensation of Beau trailing his fingers down her body, massaging its folds and crevices. As the steam enveloped her, it was easy to picture his naked, well-muscled body surrounding hers. She leaned against the smooth lava stone shower, wondering whether his skin would be rough like the stone or smooth like marble. Nearly moaning, she decided enough was enough and decreased the water temperature to bring herself out of the steamy interlude she had created. *Whoa Nelly, get a grip on yourself. I'll see the man on Sunday and get over this silliness. I don't need him.* While she did not need Beau, her body wanted to feel his touch, to kiss his lips, to taste his skin.

She didn't *want* to want Beau. Certainly not a man as arrogant and smug as he. Why was she spending so much time fantasizing about him? Why couldn't she get him out of her thoughts? And what on earth was she going to wear tonight?

As she wrapped the eggplant plush bath sheet around her, she used the lavender-scented body lotion. She tried like the devil not to imagine Beau applying it on her—if she did say so herself—still in good shape body. She felt happy about her healthy toned California-tanned body. While she was no Miss America, she did manage to turn heads despite her fifty-one years. She looked down her body as she donned her hot pink high-cut briefs, liking how they made her legs appear longer. She exchanged the bath sheet for a purple robe, gathered her things, and returned to her cabin to apply her makeup and get dressed for the evening.

She pulled out a sleeveless sundress, held it to her body, rejected it, then grabbed the jumpsuit from the hanger, holding it to her shoulders. She peered into the full-length mirror before ultimately grabbing her black jeans and white shirt, adding gold hoops to her ears. Just in case she looked too prim and proper, she left the top two buttons of her blouse open, displaying only a slight bit of cleavage. To draw the eye downward, she wore a teardrop ruby necklace. She decided to use eyeshadow to give her a smoky look and wore her red open-toed strappy sandals. Grabbing a red clutch, she left.

Eve decided to take the Gatlinburg trolley to town, which regularly stopped at the Lodge. "Will this trolley take me to Baily's?" she asked the driver.

"It does. Be sure to get off at Airport Road."

The trolley driver apparently noticed Eve's uneasiness.

"You're new here, aren't cha? Not to worry. Just look up. When you see the Space Needle, you get off. The trolley runs until eleven on weekends."

Eve hadn't been to town on her own yet. She had flown in, and her father and his wife, Marsha, had picked her up at the airport. They drove back to the Lodge through Wears Valley Road. They hadn't gone through Gatlinburg.

She had no idea Parkway Road was lined with arcades, souvenir shops, boutiques, crafters shops, and restaurants. You name it, Gatlinburg had it. The trolley passed pockets of cute little shops and some restaurants with patios that opened to the river, which appeared more of a stream than a river.

Eve managed to get off the trolley at the right location and spotted Baily's on the right-hand side of the road. She entered on the street level and found Sunny, who was wearing—what else?—a sunny yellow off-the-shoulder sundress.

Sunny ushered her through the throng and pushed her up a stairway. "You're going to love this place."

"Sunny, this place is a bar!"

"No, it's not. It's a pub."

"Same difference."

"Is not."

"Is too."

Eve couldn't help but giggle along with her half-sister.

"I knew you'd fit into the Weathers family just fine," Sunny said.

They entered through saloon-type doors.

"What are you drinking?" Sunny asked.

Eve frowned in thought as she reviewed choices. "A Strawberry Margarita."

Sunny disappeared, and Eve worked her way to the side of the room. The setup of the pub was strange. There were half a dozen high tables with two equally towering chairs placed across from one another. Each table sported a numbered placard marked *reserved*. She wondered where Sunny and she would hang.

People seemed to be just standing around. There appeared to be quite a few men milling about the place, and she hoped they weren't in a gay bar by mistake. Most of the men were worth looking at twice. She kept her gaze down and startled when Sunny placed the drink in front of her.

"Give me your credit card," Sunny demanded.

"Sure, no problem. I'd have given it to you to begin with, but you're in such a hurry…" Eve was beginning to wonder even more about Sunny.

"The charge is thirty-five dollars."

"That's either some fantastic Margarita or a very pricey cover charge."

"It's neither. It's for charity." Sunny smiled absently and seemed to be scanning the crowd as if waiting for something or someone.

"Excuse me?" Eve asked.

"I'll be right back, and I'll explain everything. You're going to love my genius plan. I got this."

And that's precisely why I'm worried. You got what, exactly? Eve did as directed while Sunny hurried off toward the bar, her wavy hair bouncing behind her. The crowd around Eve now pressed against the edge of the dancefloor, where the reserved tables were set up.

When Sunny returned, she said, "Keep an eye on your drink. Don't accept *any* from anyone, you hear?"

Eve quirked an eyebrow. "What am I, sixteen? I've been to a bar before. I'm not about to let anyone roofie my drinks."

The recessed lights dimmed, and spotlights shone over the six tables, highlighting them. The crowd grew quiet.

Before Eve could register what was going on, Sunny spoke in a rush. "Okay. This event is a charity to support the *Saint Mary's Single Seniors Association*."

Eve spat out a mouthful of her drink. "*Senior* Singles! What?"

Sunny patted her on the shoulder. "Relax. Trust me." She walked to the center of the floor, and a spotlight shone on her. She took the mic and tapped it to say, "Testing, one, two… Testing…" Noting the sound was clear, she began. "Good evening, everyone, and welcome to The Senior Singles Speediest Speed Dating Night. As you may know, I'm Sunny Days, and I'm no longer single and not a senior. But I am the Social Chairperson for Events at the Sugarlands, who are co-sponsoring tonight's event. The proceeds go to our Outreach Program for Wounded Veterans. There'll be six five-minute stops of getting to know a potential date. I'll let you know when to rotate. Here's how this works. You have to be single. Obviously."

The audience chuckled, and Sunny ignored the Captain Obvious catcalls from a few hecklers.

When the hubbub quieted, Sunny continued. "The single women will *not* rotate, but the single men will. Hopefully, the first round will be successful, but you can sign up for an additional round. Just see me. Once signed in, no skipping tables, and no slipping out of the round.

"Ladies, please wear your nametag—first names only—and table number. Gents, you'll rotate clockwise through tables to meet candidates one through six. Everyone, please be sure to fill out and return the contact information form. Write down the name of the person you're *dating*. Place a check in the column next to the person's name if you'd like to see them again for a more traditional date. If you'd like to contact that person, and your preferences match, we will notify you tomorrow by six in the evening. Then you two are on your own.

"However," Sunny voice rose and became playful. "Those who can't wait that long—you all know who you are—nothing stops you from going downstairs to the restaurant and having dinner. Good luck. Smile. I'll call table assignments now. Ida Mae, table one, Jo Ellen, table two, Bitsy Lee, table three, Eve, table four…"

The rest of the names went by Eve in a rush. She couldn't believe it. *Speed Dating! I'm speed dating? I'm going to kill Sunny.*

CHAPTER FOUR: BRING BACK THOSE SUNNY DAYS

Eve fumed but sat at her assigned table and glared at her sister.

Sunny smiled back and set the timer. "Ready. Set. Date."

Instantly, Eve found herself face-to-face with a decent looking man who was neither balding nor fat. His blue eyes danced as he extended his hand to shake hers. "I must have died and gone to heaven."

"Huh?"

"Because I'm pretty sure you're an angel who fell from above so we could meet. I'm Drake Bowles, and you're…"

Before Eve could bite her tongue, she blurted, "Ready to kill my sister."

"That sounds pretty extreme. What did she do?"

"She didn't tell me about this speed dating thing. I had no idea!"

Drake rocked back in his seat, fiddling with his beer label. "I like long walks on the beach, do you?"

"Nope."

"What? I thought all women like long romantic walks."

"Not me. It's tiring walking on sand. Waves get your feet wet and then all sandy. I like sitting on a lounge chair under an umbrella, sipping a mai tai."

"What *do* you like?"

"The sound of a timer going off."

Then the timer went off, and Sunny called out, "Gentlemen, please move to the next table."

"Bye. Nice to meetcha, Drake," Eve murmured, waving. *I'm coming off like a blithering idiot. I am so not prepared for this. I hate feeling out of control, and this is out of my depth.*

The next man who graced her table was easy on the eyes. But she kept focusing on his toupee. She considered bolting, but this *was* a fundraiser for a worthy cause, so she was able to offer him some sort of smile.

He was looking at her like a deer in the headlights and stumbled over himself. "Do you realize your twin is up there hosting this event for single folks? Storme Knight, you are a *married* woman. What do you think you're doing?" He was getting redder in the face by the minute.

Eve worried he'd have a coronary.

Fortunately, Sunny called out a time-out and explained Eve was, in fact, *not* Storme but was *family*. Unfortunately, the mic was open, so her status and existence were broadcast to all the patrons. The man — whose name she never caught — yelled *Do-over*, but Sunny wisely rotated the men once more.

Eve took a big gulp of her drink and glowered at Sunny, who demonstrated good sense by bringing her another drink. Eve prayed it was good and strong. She picked up the cocktail napkin and fanned herself, trying to regain her composure. *I'd better not get a hot flash from all this stress. That's all I need.*

"Come here often?" the next man asked.

"Nope. Never been here before."

The guy's next question was at least easy to answer. "What would you miss most if you were stranded on a desert island?"

"Toilet paper."

His mouth sprang open and stayed that way.

Oops. Shoulda thought more about that answer. Good thing I'm not really here to meet anyone. I suck at this.

Eve crossed her fingers. Three down, three to go.

The man flushed and tried again. His hands flung out, indicating their surroundings. "Why are we here?"

She frowned. *Is this guy crazy?* "Uh, apparently to meet someone?"

"No, I mean, why are we on this planet?"

Eve just gaped at him. "Cuz we were born here, not on Jupiter?"

He looked disappointed. "I'm Sam Addams. You may have noticed I take a philosophical look at things. I'm a student of life, and I'm interested in studying you."

Fortunately, the buzzer went off. Eve shifted on her stool, crossed and re-crossed her legs, then fiddled with her cocktail napkin once more. *At this rate, it'll be in shreds in no time.*

The next man was a total knockout in the looks department. "Have we met before?"

"Nada, I just arrived here recently." She actually blushed for no good reason.

He smiled at her and winked. "Hey, you're pretty, and I'm cute. Together we'd be pretty cute."

Eve cocked her head and lifted a brow. "Does that line usually work for ya? Just wondering."

He looked confused by her response and shrugged his shoulders. "Yeah, actually in most cases I get a smile and an introduction."

"Hmm. I see."

They were interrupted by the next rotation. Eve drummed her fingers. *That fourth exchange was the best so far.* Eve let out a breath she hadn't fully realize she'd been holding.

She felt the presence of the next one before she could see him. When she looked up, it was to find deep gray eyes full of amusement, smiling at her.

"Fancy meeting you here," Beau Jobs said in that velvety voice she recognized.

Eve swallowed hard and struggled to find her voice. Failing, she took another swig of her heavily liquored concoction. *Thank heaven this is strong.* She pulled herself together. Her face heated. "What are you doing here? I thought you were done—and I quote—*looking for love in all the wrong places.*"

His eyes twinkled. "Who said this is the wrong place?"

"I didn't expect you to be here."

He nodded. "Likewise. But I bet I know how we each got here."

In unison, they said, "Sunny."

Despite herself, she laughed. "Look, Beau, this is so embarrassing. I swear I didn't put Sunny up to this."

"Of that, I have no doubt. We really started out on the wrong foot at the Lodge. I was there to hook—"

She stopped him with an upraised palm. "Let's not go back there. I get it."

The timer went off, but before he got up, he leaned over and whispered, "Later."

She watched Beau saunter to the table and had just enough time to note how good he looked in his stylish khaki-colored jacket worn over a black shirt and slacks. *Oh my, what a mighty fine ass he has on him.*

Eve was still recovering from Beau's presence when the next candidate joined her. The guy must have been sixty, but he was on the sunny side of it. He made a good first impression. "You from Tennessee?"

Before she could even answer, he continued. "Because you are the only *ten* I see in here."

The conversation went nowhere fast. It trickled to nothing as the long minutes dragged on.

The first round ended as the timer went off. Sunny was at the mic again. "We'll take a five-minute breather. You can nab an appetizer and a fresh drink, then the next round will start."

Eve ducked aside to make a quick exit. She hadn't signed up for another round, so technically, she wasn't breaking any speed dating rules.

Excited eager singles fought their way toward hopeful suitors while grabbing fried pickles and other munchies. In the milling crowd, Eve spied an opening to sneak out of Baily's from the second floor. She made a beeline for the stairs. When the pressing crowd pitched her perilously close to a serious fall, a pair of strong arms caught and held her close to a solid chest.

She couldn't escape the clean man smell nor her body's reaction to it. A sharp zing coursed through her. *What the hell!* For an instant, she wanted to remain in those stranger's arms...like maybe forever.

"Steady, there." The voice rumbled, full of concern and security.

She accepted his help. "I'm fine."

Eve knew that voice. It was Beau. Again.

He steadied her as she tottered on her strappy heels.

His eyes traversed her frame as she regained her footing, but they were blocking the way. He took her by the elbow, steering her toward a table. "Are you all right?"

His smooth tone helped her regain her balance — physical and emotional. Then his hands moved with sureness over her body.

"What the hell are you doing?" She brushed his searching fingers away.

"Checking you for injuries, broken bones..."

"I said I was fine." She sank into the barrel chair, thankful for the supporting arms of the man — not that she'd ever admit it — and the chair. Though she was not ready to deal with Beau or her reaction to him.

Quick as a bee sting, he stopped. "So, sue me if I'm a good Christian man."

Her mouth hung open. "Say what?"

"You've heard of the Good Samaritan?"

She drew out her words. "Yes…of course…"

"I'm just doing a good deed. Let's go downstairs to Baily's restaurant to get some food in you. It'll help to soak up the alcohol, restore you, and rebuild your tissues."

She gaped at him. "Rebuild my tissues? What? Are you for real?" But she was hungry.

"You need something more than fried pickles in you if you even made it to the hors d'oeuvres. Let's get you something worthwhile to eat."

"Thanks. I was trying to escape."

The light danced in his eyes. "But I caught you."

She smiled, a tad embarrassed. "Normally, I'm not so clumsy."

"Looks like a happy accident. Imagine bumping into you twice in one night. It must be a sign."

"Yeah, a clear sign I'm going to kill my sister for putting me in this position."

He chuckled. "I like the position you're in. Let's get you out of this crowd. I'm just doing a good deed."

She gaped at him. "For real?"

"I was an Eagle Scout with a basic knowledge of First Aid." He crossed his heart and then held up three fingers in a boy scout salute. "As such, I'd never cop a feel."

She raised a brow, skeptical. "Have you always been such a choir boy? I see you were definitely…prepared."

He buffed his fingernails on his chest. "Choir boy? Hardly. But *always be prepared*. That's the scout motto."

"Are you always a boy scout, then?"

"That remains to be seen." The twinkle in his eyes now seemed more of a delicious glint. "Now how about a burger. They're the best in town."

She conceded. "I could use one. Smells great in here. Want to share onion rings?" *Maybe the onions will keep him at bay and keep his hands away. Hmm, maybe I should rethink that. Those were great hands.*

21

Their banter continued as she ate the best burger she'd ever had. "Mm, these are good," she murmured as the juices dripped on her fingers.

He lifted a finger to her lips, swiped the juices there, and sucked his fingers. He winked. "Mighty tasty."

She felt the heat rise in her cheeks, so she glanced around the dining area, which had begun to fill as they ate.

When the check came, he waved away her attempts to pay. "I've got this. After all, I did ask you to stay."

Eve allowed it. "Thanks. I owe you one."

He rose and helped her out of the chair. As he escorted her out, he paused and asked, "Wait. Is this a date?"

Eve raised a brow. "Is it Sunday morning?"

"No."

"Then it's no date. Our date is set for Sunday, remember? If you'll excuse me, I have to catch the trolley home. I don't want to miss it."

"I'll drive you."

"No need. You've done enough for one day."

"At least let me wait with you."

Eve smiled and nodded.

They walked to the stop, talking of insignificant things. The night was gentle and warm. His thigh touched hers when he sat next to her on the bench, and she did not shift away.

When the trolley arrived, he gave her a small salute and strode off into the night, heading toward the Ripley Aquarium Parking Structure.

Eve boarded the trolley and sat in the open section at the back, savoring her thoughts. A soft smile stole across her face.

She thought about his dreamy gray eyes. Thought of the set of his shoulders and the way he seemed to just exude strength and protection. Thought of how the material of his slacks stretched tight over a fine man-frame. Thought how not every man would wait with her for a trolley. She was so caught up remembering his clean, woodsy, manly scent that when the trolley reached the Lodge in no time, she was shocked. But still, even as she walked through the forest to her cabin, she couldn't quite get him out of her mind. *Maybe I was too quick to turn down his offer to drive me back. Would he have kissed me? I'd be up for that. Perhaps he'd be* up *too.* She chuckled.

Chapter Five: Sunday Morning Sunshine

Eve dressed carefully but practically for Mass and her date with Beau. True, they were going to church and afterward would help with the ongoing Pancake Breakfast, but she still wanted to look good. She wore a long denim skirt and a short-sleeved red striped shirt. Taming her mass of curls and waves would do no good, but she tried.

She borrowed Samson—Storme's car—and drove to St. Mary's. She left the parking lot and went to the front of the church to meet Beau.

Beau smiled in greeting when he met her outside and held the heavy church door open for her. They entered, genuflected, and took seats in a pew near the altar. Beau had stepped aside to let her proceed him into the pew, then sat nearest to the aisle.

As the processional—led by an altar girl carrying the crucifix on a long pole—came down the aisle, Eve's hands touched Beau's when they both reached for the same hymnal. Electricity sped through her. *Yikes!* She had a hard time joining in the opening hymn because the strength of the zing rocked her senses.

"Let us greet each other in fellowship. Turn now and extend yourselves to God's people," Father Dale intoned. People shifted right and left, greeting each other. "Let us sing."

Beau held the hymnal for both of them to use and winked at her, and her *damned* pulse just sang in tune. Things went from bad to worse each time they touched. She swore she was shaking with the heat of it.

Shit! I just swore in church, and oops, I did it again. Sorry, God. Eve recovered from his touch and did well dealing with her suddenly horny self, getting through the sermon and offertory. Until her thigh touched his when she preceded him to get communion. It was hard to think godly thoughts after that. And later, during the sign of peace, instead of shaking her hand, he kissed her lips, and she nearly lost it. She hated how strongly her body reacted to his. It knocked her off-kilter, made her feel inept, kept her insides spinning.

Beau's clear, strong tones rang out as he sang *A Mighty Fortress* as Mass ended. *Wow. This guy can sing! Note to self, remind me to challenge him to a karaoke night. Not that I want to go out with him. Just to prove I can sing. It's just this sudden, uh, frog in my throat that prevents me from joining the chorus. Praise God, the Mass is just about over.*

Thank God, that's over. Never had such a hard time concentrating. Eve was a temptation that got worse by the minute throughout the service. From the moment I met her, I can't seem to stop thinking about her. My focus is supposed to be on my company, not this cool cucumber. Something about her says go away while her eyes beg me to come hither. Don't know what's so different about her. All I have to do is get through this pancake ordeal and then I can go home and look at my spreadsheets. I didn't know acquiring this communications business was going to be so complicated. Sure as hell hadn't banked on Eve.

The fact was the business was not that challenging. Beau had made it so by insisting on performing every component, from selling, installation, connections, and maintenance. That meant he experienced what the cable guys in the field actually did. He was a hands-on person with business administration and marketing in his background. *I never want to ask an employee to do something I haven't done myself.*

That obstinacy had put him in his ex-wife's crosshairs. Deborah hadn't understood his business model or mentality—didn't want to and never had. She just wanted to spend the results of his hard work. She didn't like the sacrifice, especially when she felt *she* was the sacrifice. *Maybe she was, maybe she wasn't. By the time we divorced, we were both broken.*

He wrestled with his past, his present, and his fascination with Eve. He had responded to a call from Sky Scraper, the Lodge's COO, and they had settled on what the Lodge needed and what his company would offer. She had signed off on the deal, yet here he was dealing with Eve Windsong instead. And therein lay the rub. They hadn't started out on the right foot, and now he was going to church and agreeing to help out at a pancake breakfast. How in hell had that happened? *She thinks I'm just the cable guy, not the Garter Bytes Communications System* owner. *Oh well, it's not like I'm gonna marry her or anything. Let her think what she wants.*

Eve led Beau toward the stairway down into the church basement's temporary social hall. As she swung through the kitchen area, she grabbed two aprons and threw one his way. He caught it and wore it with apparent pride.

"Hope you really can flip a pancake," she teased. She introduced Beau to Luke Scraper along with the rest of the crew, announcing, "I brought you help so you can go home to your quads."

Luke wasted no time. He shucked his apron, and with a broad gesture, said, "Have at. You ever worked a griddle before?"

Beau nodded. "I was in the military and on KP often enough. I can manage." He picked up the spatula and began flipping like an expert, sending some sky-high and catching them like a pro.

Eve started mixing the next batch. Her tongue protruded slightly as she concentrated, trying to be careful when she measured ingredients. Before long, she had flour in her hair and batter on her cheek. Beau reached over and flicked the smudge from her cheek, and it felt as if scorch marks followed the path of his finger.

His touch seemed to ignite her.

The rhythm of the kitchen proved a good antidote to her troublesome hormones, though she still felt the heat from the proximity of their bodies. People chitchatted as they worked. True to his word, Beau *could* flip a flapjack. *Hm. Fancy that. Each flip showed a fine-honed bicep and triceps that are praiseworthy.* The rippling muscles were fun to watch. She wished she could stare, but she was busy. At least she was supposed to be.

Eve noticed Sunny grabbing an apron to begin her shift. "I'm going to strangle you!"

Beau flipped a pancake high this time but was obviously distracted by Sunny. He failed to catch the half-cooked flapjack, and it landed on Eve. She was dripping with semi-cooked batter. As she recovered from her shock, she noticed his shoulders shaking with laughter. She grabbed a gob of the pancake mixture and sent it sailing his way. It caught his shoulder. Some more batter dripped down her face, so she scraped it off and lobbed it his way.

Then they attacked Sunny until she was covered in flour and batter.

"That'll teach you to meddle and dabble in matchmaking," Eve said.

Sunny returned fire. "Will not."

Eve let lose a ladleful. "Will too."

Others from the cooking crew ducked. Then an ear-splitting sound filled the air and hurt their ears. The smoke detector blurted as the kitchen filled with smoke from some pancakes burning on the griddle. The other volunteer cooks shoed the three of them away and tossed them towels to clean up their act.

Millie, the Lodge cook, clucked around them like a wet hen. "You've made a mess."

"Truce," Beau called as he waved a towel in surrender.

"You two are acting like some characters in a Hallmark Movie," Millie groused.

"Yeah," someone else said. "Get a room."

On his way out of the kitchen, Beau grabbed a banana.

Beau and Eve doubled over, laughing. Beau dabbed at her hair, trying to undo the damage. It was hopeless.

Sunny took that moment to bug out.

"You owe me breakfast," Eve said.

He handed her the banana and winked. "I was gonna make you my famous blackberry and banana pancakes before we closed the kitchen down. But since I couldn't, how about a do-over?"

"It isn't blackberry season yet. As tempting as that is, I think I deserve more than to risk stepping into a kitchen with you again. You can take me to the Pancake Pantry in the Village Shoppes on Parkway for the real deal."

"It's a date."

CHAPTER SIX: WORKING NINE TO FIVE

Monday was the first day that Eve was on her own at the Lodge. Storme would be around, but Skye, whose place she was taking, would be at home tending to her brood. Eve did not envy that task.

She knew her father and his wife helped out on occasion, but they each had their own business as well. John spent time in his woodcraft shop and then relieved Marsha so she could run her apothecary.

Eve's reason to substitute for Skye was rooted in two factors. She genuinely wanted to help her long-lost half-sister and her quadruplets. Equally, she also yearned to get to know her father. He'd had no idea that her mother, Mariah Windsong, had become pregnant during their Woodstock hookup. To say their encounter shook up the family was an understatement. Apparently, though John was an only child, he'd created twins twice with the only two women he'd had sex with.

Eve learned most about her father by how he treated her half-siblings and his grandchildren. She could understand his connection to them and nurtured a hope that she could be more than just a shock to his system. She had at least the summer to get to know him. He seemed to be a real artisan. If there wasn't a baby in his arms, there was a carving knife and wood between his adept fingers.

She was in conference with Storme about yesterday's business numbers and could barely spare time to acknowledge

Beau's presence at the Lodge. Cables and cords, wires and men, wound their way through the establishment. They exchanged greetings on the fly with smiles and nods.

Eve went to have lunch in the Lodge's Dining Room when she was interrupted by that rich voice she was quickly learning to love. "This seat taken?"

She looked up at Beau and smiled in invitation. "It is now. Pull up a chair."

"This job's a bit bigger than I anticipated."

"Oh?"

"Skye told me this Lodge served as an emergency relief center in case of any natural disaster, or in this case a possible shut down."

Eve was startled. "What do you mean?"

"Yeah, this Lodge provided shelter for displaced folks during the Chimney Tops Two Wildfire of 2016 and became a refuge in what we call Snowmageddon about a year or two later."

Eve huffed her surprise. "Wow, what a giving family I've stumbled into."

It was Beau's turn to look confused.

"Long story."

He laughed. "Where have I heard that before?"

"Why did the job get larger?"

"Heard the news lately on the radio or television?"

"Not really. Working here keeps me out in these beautiful hills. Not good reception. Isn't that why you're here? I'm busy learning hotel management, and there are no TVs except in the office and Great Room, and they're not in use now, thanks to you."

Beau shoved his hat on the back of his head, stretched to give his long legs more room, and sipped sweet tea from the Mason jar she had poured for him. He placed his order and then said. "There's some new virus, coronavirus, from China that could have folks in a dither. I'm doing some additional modifications, adding bandwidth, that kind of thing, in case you need to house folks. Communication systems are vital. You need to be prepared."

His order arrived as Eve finished hers. She ordered them both peach cobblers and grew pensive. "That's sobering news."

His smile was grim. "The good news is the Lodge will be state of the art, and you'll be in touch. Actually, the Center for Disease Control, the CDC, advises against touching, but you have got to be informed. Now more than ever."

Eve stood up. "You've given me a lot to think about. If you'll excuse me, I've got some preparing to do. I have to talk with Skye, Sunny, and Storme."

"Sit down. Eat your cobbler. Let me arrange a GoToMeeting online meeting."

"You've got that far already?"

"Not as far as I'd like, but I can set that function up long enough to do what you need. Tell the trio I highly recommend you outfit — temporarily, of course — some cabins with TVs in case of quarantine. That way, people can be informed and entertained."

"I'm going out on a limb here — executive decision. Do that. Equip the Family cottages and second floor rooms. Now, about that conference call..."

Beau finished his cobbler and then escorted Eve to the office, where he literally made the hookup.

Storme was already at the office, so once Skye and Sunny joined the call, they overruled Sunny's protests that her advertisements had to be altered. Eve reassured Sunny, "I didn't mean connect *all* the rooms. Just the cabins and a few rooms in case we have to become a relief center or — God forbid, a field hospital."

Skye gasped. "Do you think it'll get that bad? Is it that serious?"

"Nobody knows, but a wise man we hired suggested we be prepared."

Sunny's voice bounced with untampered glee. "Would that certain someone just happen to be installing our communications system? Looks like you're doing some connecting of your own."

Eve tempered her growing impatience with Sunny. "Maybe it does. Maybe it doesn't."

Sunny squealed. "Operation Senior Sex is a go."

Flushing deeply, hoping the noise of the electric drill drowned Sunny's suggestive words, Eve secured their approval and owned up to her executive decision.

"Fifty isn't a senior anything, ya know. All it gets you is freedom and AARP membership."

Sunny preened and crowed, "I don't even know what that means, but if you know, then I rest my case. Buh-bye."

Skye affirmed that and signed off as well.

"Eve, you didn't have to fess up about your decision, ya know, you made the right call," Storme whispered.

"Best to be upfront. Even though the damage was done." Eve gestured about the room at the paraphernalia that littered the office. "It's pretty evident that I acted without official sanction."

Storme nodded. "Better to beg forgiveness than ask permission. I'll put in an order for a dozen thirty-six-inch flat-screens. We'll get the local business discount and faster service that way."

The sound of coil, cable, and drilling made further conversation futile, so Eve went back to work.

In the office, Eve turned CNN on low to keep up with the news. China seemed to be the area of concern, not North America. Nonetheless, she told Millie to stock up on both food and cleaning products. *Always be prepared.* Beau's words echoed clearly in her mind. He had announced he was going to inspect the cabins, which stood in a well-spaced semi-circle behind the Lodge.

She didn't see much of Beau the rest of the day, but he was never far from her thoughts. Her body hummed in expectant surges of restrained but acknowledged passion.

The creek flowed behind or beside many cabins, depending on its many twists and turns. Eve liked to sit beside it after she finished her shift. Her mind replayed the times her skin had touched Beau's, and she shivered in delight. *Maybe Sunny's right. It might be kind of fun getting in touch with my sensual side. And Beau is a better candidate than any of the Mountain-Match.com men. And far better than the other senior speed daters.*

She enjoyed the fresh, clean scent of the cedar and hickory in her surroundings. Spring was in the air. The play of sunlight, catching the tumbling water as it coursed through the rock-strewn brook, was mountain scenery at its best. Birdsong filled the breeze, and she wondered about kissing Beau. His lips begged to be kissed. Would his lips be hot? Firm? Soft with passion? Rough with desire? Wet? She hoped they were all of the above.

The sound of sticks cracking broke the silence. Her hand flew to her chest to cover her rapidly beating heart. *Bear? Dear God! Wild Animal?*

Beau emerged from the forest, gestured at a greyback, and asked, "This rock taken?" He sat his rugged-self next to her and placed his tools on the bank.

Eve scooted over to put some much-needed space between them. Her heart beat like a drum, and the blood rushing through her veins sounded like thunder in her ears.

"Don't sneak up on me like that! You nearly gave me a heart attack."

"What that?" He grinned. Then he lowered his lips to hers

and kissed her. *"That* is what should make your heart attack-worthy, not me walking down the path."

"Oh yeah." She raised her brow, grabbed his face, and tilted her head. "This is a heart attack kiss." She ran her tongue around his mouth, thoroughly enjoying his wet, sweet lips. Her blood raced through her suddenly hot body. She leaned closer, seeking, desiring, and wanting more. Then sanity reared its head, and she pulled back. "What are we doing?"

"Whatever we're doing, I don't want to stop."

"What if the work crew or worse Sunny catches us?"

"Buzzkill." He got up, held out a hand, and raised her to her feet. "That kiss was a long time coming."

"How so?"

"Ever since I came to hook up your system, I wanted to kiss you."

"About that." Eve had to set the record straight. "Sunny talked me into joining MountainMatch.com, and it's so hard to write about myself… Long story short, *she* wrote and posted my profile, and since then, I've had a long line of men contacting me."

"And you thought I was there to virtually hookup. Oh, my God! No wonder you reacted like you did."

They continued walking until they reached his truck. "Look, why don't you meet me at No Way Jose's on the river, and you can tell me all the lines you heard and the dates you had. We'll see how I stack up."

"It's a date. Seven o'clock tonight?"

He nodded and walked with her to his service van.

Eve shivered, enjoying the tingle that went through her when he kissed goodbye. *Fancy that. His kiss was much better after I showed him how I want to be kissed. Fast learner.* Then she made her way to the Spa Haus, enjoyed a warm, wonderful shower, and topped that off with a trip to the sauna nearby.

Then she really went for gold and simmered in the luxurious hot tub, enjoying the jets caressing her body. She was a limp as a wet noodle when she dried off.

When she reached Little Miss Muffet's cabin, she saw the sawdust in the wastebasket that told her Beau had been in her room. *Wonder what he thought about my leopard-print bra and bikini panties?* Her body heated. She'd wear the push-up bra and panties for tonight's date. *Oh My God! A date! I'm going on a date…with a hot cable guy.*

Beau swallowed. *How the hell did that happen? That kiss knocked my fuckin' socks off. I wasn't aiming for that. She looked so sweet. A sweet little nothing kiss was all I was after. Those leopard-print panties… Who knew underneath that frosty façade lay a seething lava stream of pure molten woman with a capital W. Good Lord, I feel like a motherfuckin' teenager. I'm fifty-five, for God's sake.* He smiled. *Fifty is the new thirty…gotta keep that in mind. Damn, now I have a hard-on!*

CHAPTER SEVEN: THE LION ROARS TO-NIGHT

Eve wore a short skirt and an ice-blue tank top, which coordinated well with a pert scarf that drew attention to her deep blue eyes. Her sister and half-sisters shared the same eyes. *Those eyes are obviously an inherited trait , because the Quad Squad share them as well.*

She walked to the veranda, where the trolley typically waited in the semi-circle gravel road that hemmed the front lawn. She loved the front yard Wishing Well and tossed in some change for luck. She heard the sound of an engine before she saw the car. Her brows shot skyward when the vehicle came into view. *Wow, nice wheels. And the driver screams sex-on-a-stick, too. Wait. Is that Beau? What's he doing here?*

The late afternoon sun lit the car, and she could see her reflection in its flawless paint job. "Nice wheels."

"You like?"

"What's not to like? A midnight blue classic convertible Caddy is sweet."

"It's a hit at Thursday's Classic Car Circuit in Pigeon Forge, and believe it or not, I like to cruise the Parkway in Gatlinburg on Saturday nights."

"No way! Get out of here. No, you don't!"

"I do. I'll take you Saturday, and you can see for yourself. I'd get you for Thursday, but we show all day, and I'm tied up with car buffs. But..." he snapped his fingers. "You can catch the trolley to Pigeon Forge. Not sure if the purple line goes that far, but for sure, there's a line that does."

Eve looked at him. She was puzzled but smiled. "Did I get my wires crossed? Wasn't I supposed to meet you at Jose's? Yet here you are."

He laughed. "I know where you're staying. I thought you'd enjoy a ride."

Eve raised a hand to shade her eyes, since the sunlight was so bright. She smiled, and with a teasing tone, she said, "Maybe I like trolley rides."

"I dare you to pass up this ride." He opened the car door.

She slid onto the seat, careful to keep her skirt from riding up. She noticed the beautiful white leather seats. "You even have seatbelts! I didn't know classic cars had them."

"Not all cars did. But this is a Cadillac, a 1969 Cadillac de Ville. It came with a standard V8 engine. Seatbelts were also standard. Buckle up."

The wheels spun gravel as Beau gunned the engine, and they made their way — top down — to No Way Jose's.

Eve ordered a mojito to enjoy with her steak fajitas. The sautéed vegetables alone could easily have made a meal. However, she'd miss the delicious, freshly made tortillas. She was sure by the end of the meal she would be full, but not completely satisfied. *I'm almost certain he could easily satisfy my every appetite.* She chided herself mentally for her equally delicious thoughts.

Above the aroma of the Mexican food, she detected a citrus aftershave that competed for her attention. Her hands shook as she lifted the fajita to her lips. She caught the steak juices with the tip of her tongue and savored the flavor.

Beau's gaze devoured her as he tracked the path of her tongue. He shifted in his chair, cleared his throat, and dug into the chimichanga he'd ordered. When he bit into it, pleasure crossed his face, and soft appreciative moans suggested he enjoyed it. "Tell me about your MountainMatch.com dating experience."

Eve was in the process of sipping her drink when he asked. She grabbed her napkin and held it to her lips to prevent spitting it all over their meal. "Pardon me." She chuckled. "It's been a trip. No guy matched his photo. The photos were at least twenty years younger and thirty pounds lighter than whoever showed up. One actually brought a hand puppet named Pepe. It interrupted what little conversation I could muster. Pepe called me a cock tease."

It was Beau's turn to burst into laughter and scramble to cover his mouth. "You're kidding me!"

"I kid you not. I threw some money on the table, said we weren't a match, and hightailed it out of there. Fortunately, I had Samson."

Beau looked at her and straightened in his seat. "Samson? You brought Samson with you? Who's he?"

Was Beau jealous?

"Wait. No." She couldn't help but smile. "Storme named her car Samson. She lent it to me."

She leaned forward, resting her face on both hands, cupping her chin. "Another guy, after a wonderful evening at the theater and a lovely dinner, told me the walls at his place looked like someone vomited all over them. Then he invited me in to—get this—give him decorating advice! Needless to say, I declined. He drove me straight back to the Lodge, said I was a big girl, and dropped me off under a streetlight at the bottom of the driveway. And I was wearing heels too!"

"He did not!" Beau gaped. "That driveway is rocky. Gravel is too kind a word for it. What'd you do?"

She showed him. She raised her finger and gave him the bird.

Beau laughed outright.

Eve was so miffed by the memory she felt heat flooding her

cheeks. "All I could see was that weak veranda lantern piercing the darkness. There could have been a wolf or a bear…"

"Sounds like *he* was a wolf."

"Yup."

Beau's gray eyes sparkled. "No wonder you were upset when I said I'd hook you up."

She laughed. "I thought you were another MountainMatch.com man. That may have been the worst line I'd had heard up to that point. But enough about me. What's your story?"

"Not much to tell. Football. College scholarship. Divorced. One teenaged son, Jake."

"Oh?"

He sighed. "The divorce tore me up pretty bad. She got custody. That hurt. But I was away on business a lot, and she didn't like it. Said I cared about work, not them. They're in Nashville, and I'm here working." He shrugged. "That just reinforced her thinking. Why stop working hard now? The damage has been done. I hate knowing they're my casualties. My fault, but not solely my heartache."

Eve felt for him. She saw the regret and pain in his gaze. "You probably thought you were building a future for all of you. You do the best you can with what you know at the time. Who knew?" She extended her hand across the table to touch his, offering her sympathy.

Fire from the skin on skin contact leaped between them. Eve withdrew her hand quickly with a light laugh. "Oops. Sorry no touching."

He raised his eyes in question. "Says who?"

She grinned. "From what you told me, the CDC and WHO, World Health Organization, that's who."

"What do they know?"

Chapter Eight: Can't Stop the Feel-ing

After dinner, Eve enjoyed their stroll on Parkway, pausing to watch the wild ducks float in the swift river current. They could have gone down the part of Parkway where the bright lights of the boutiques and stores beckoned, or even down Little River Road along the streamline river. Yet their peaceful stroll seemed a perfect choice.

The full moon lit their way, and the early spring breeze off the river made her shiver. Beau took off his sports jacket and draped it around her shoulders. She snuggled into it. His citrusy smell assaulted her senses, and she wanted to bury herself not only within its folds but also in him. They walked farther and then sat on a bench facing the river. A mother duck, leading some downy fur balls, streamed down the river.

Beau chuckled as they struggled out of the water to the bank. The mother adeptly used her beak to gently nudge a not quite ready duckling to safety, then huddled her young beneath her wings.

She and Beau stood for a better view, neither of them making a sound. Then Beau raised her face, lacing his fingers through her hair, and kissed her slowly.

Hand in hand, he led her back to his Cadillac. He drove the bypass back and exited at the park entrance. The cool breeze was chilly with the top down. He reached the Lodge, drove up the driveway, and parked beside Little Miss Muffet's cabin.

Eve paused for a moment, then decided to go for broke. "I have no vomit on my walls, and I don't have any etchings, but I do have Ole Smoky Apple Moonshine, if you'd like a night-cap fireside."

Beau smiled. His eyes glittered in the moonlight. "Don't mind if I do."

Her hands trembled as she gathered the mini Mason jars. *You'd think I was a virgin. Geesh. It's been a while, but they say it's like riding a bike. Once you learn, you've got it. I hope he gets my message . . . This is as liberated as this woman gets.*

Eve busied herself by slipping out of his sports jacket. She draped it over a captain's chair and gestured to the fireplace. "Will you do the honors while I pour?"

He smiled at her. "Will do." He assembled the kindling, newspaper, and logs piled on the hearth, struck a match, and accepted a Mason jar full of moonshine.

Just looking at the muscles, bulging, bunching, and rippling as he moves makes me as hot as that fire. She kicked off her shoes. *I'm so wet, I'm almost embarrassed by it. I feel like it'll drip down my legs.* She sank onto the couch, since her legs were shaking with excitement.

He joined her.

Eve slipped into his arms, welcoming his warm embrace. Before long, they were making out like teenagers—except these kisses were deeper, mature, and experienced. Eve especially liked the way Beau held her head and face as he tilted it to kiss her. He wasn't greedy, but he was obviously hungry.

So was she. She met and matched his fervor.

He rained kisses over her eyelids, her ears, and the long column of her neck. When she shivered, he lingered there until she urged him onto the next spot on the opposite side.

She pulled his shirt from his slacks.

He unbuckled the belt after slipping her top off.

He kissed the crescents of her breasts that spilled above her leopard-print bra, and his tongue played with the black lace that trimmed the top. His fingers of one hand gently caressed and cupped her breasts while the other nudged her skirt down.

After successfully getting his shirt and pants off, she cuddled into him on the couch and then lifting her lips to his and kissed her way to his chest covered with fine silver hairs that curled. She ran her hands up and down his corded arms. Then she felt her bra loosen and moved to let it slip off her.

His mouth descended to lick her nipples, causing them to pucker. He stopped and returned to her lips as his hands continued to caress her breasts. Soon after, his touch skimmed down her body, sliding past her waist to rest on her hips. The fingers of one hand made their way across her labia until he reached her soaking center. He began to stroke and circle and tease until she screamed. His tongue followed his hands' lead, and he buried his face in her center.

He gently laid her down on the couch and rubbed his now throbbing cock against her nipples. His pre-cum bathed her heaving breasts as she struggled to catch her breath. *That's a new one! Whoa! Never did that before.* She liked it. Her fingers fiddled with his balls.

Then his mouth covered hers once more until she, panting and nearly begging, invited him inside. She parted her legs as he donned a condom. *Almost don't need that. I haven't had a period in a while. Caution. Danger, danger... That's how many midlife babies are conceived.*

Glad that he was sheathed, she let him enter, and when she did, she couldn't believe the fit. The rhythm. The length of him. The breadth. The rock hardness. The velvet skin covering an iron rod. The long ins and equally long outs. The gentle but rigid thrusts so slow, so measured, so right for her.

He gently rolled them off the couch to the floor. He turned her over on her side to enter her throbbing, dripping kitty. In one long, smooth stroke, he took her to the moon. *Is this what all the fuss's about! Holy Mackerel!*

She'd yearned for this moment longer than she wanted to admit. The incessant wanting that began when she took one look at him the day they met. With a few deft thrusts, she was on the precipice, and he held her there playing with both sets of lips. He nibbled and licked, kissing everywhere he could reach. His hands were skillful, with a lifetime of experience at his beck and call. She got the benefit of that. His hands busied themselves with her hair, her breasts, her back, her neck, her ears.

Eve was set to implode, then he increased his pace and thrust until they soared into the stratosphere while solar storms burst around them.

He grabbed the afghan from the sofa and drew her next to him, tucked her under his chin, cradling her as they fell into a well-earned sleep.

The sound of blackbirds awakening woke Eve as well. A smile played about her lips. She looked at the mighty fine male specimen with his tousled silver and black locks and began a gentle assault, trailing her nails up and down his well-muscled chest. She stroked his arms and played with the fine hairs she found there and then ran those same caressing fingers across the chiseled planes of his face. She ran her fingers down his back, hoping shivers went down his spine like they did hers. She got bolder and began to trace the curve of his butt when his hand shot out and grabbed her wrist.

"Mm, you smell like sex."

She giggled. "I hope it's a scent you like."

"Your scent drives me wild."

"Really?"

"Yup." He kissed her. Hard and deep. Fast.

"Show me."

He tasted her, and his need for more was clear. He rolled her on top of him. This tempo was quick. Firm. Hot. Rapid.

Wet. When he left her to find a condom, she felt cold, bereft, and lonely. Her body screamed for him. She shook with need and anticipation.

He ripped the foil packet with his teeth and grunted with barely restrained ferocity as he unfolded it.

She shot upright and helped him roll it on with shaking hands.

He growled and urged her back, parted her knees, teased her breasts, and entered. This was not gentle, but robust and rutting. They fucked like ducks. In, out, in, out. Deep thrusts. Short thrusts. Grunts. Moans escaped both throats. They were acrobats, shifting positions often. Rolling with need and passion. Thrust after thrust. Groan and moans unleashed from parched, needy, hot throats. Each took and gave as good in return until they shattered and collapsed.

She gasped. "Oh, my God! Never, have I ever…"

"Wow. Just wow."

She laughed. "We need showers."

"Lead the way."

She frowned. "We can't."

"What do you mean? We can't shower?"

"There are no showers. They're all in the Spa House. You have to go home for that, buddy."

"Yowser." He bolted up and raced into his clothes. "Gotta get out of here, pronto."

"What's the rush?"

"My big flashy car is like a neon sign, advertising your sex life. Hopefully, there aren't many early risers nearby."

She sat up. Her modesty long gone, she walked to the sink, ran the water until it was cold, and offered him a glass. "Actually, their opinion is none of my business. But perception is *reality* for some folks, and this is a small town."

"See ya later. I'm going to get ready for work."

Beau grimaced. "Christ Almighty! I'm already at work, but

no way am I ready for it."

"Good thing you live nearby. See ya around." She swatted him on his mighty fine butt.

He laughed. His job for the next few weeks was the Lodge, and she well knew it.

He gave her a salute as he left and drove off much more quietly than he'd arrived.

Chapter Nine: If You Can't Take the Heat, Get Out of the Kitchen.

Eve wasn't too concerned about getting to work on time. She generally didn't get to the main house of the Lodge until eight. Automatically, she turned on the newly installed TV.

The announcer's solemn professional voice said, "This just in. Over the course of mere weeks, cases of the highly contagious coronavirus have spread from China to Thailand, Iran, and Europe. Italy was particularly hard hit and has completely shut down. In addition, several well-known cruise lines have reported flu-like pneumonia symptoms, and the cases on board are increasing daily. Three ships have asked guests to voluntarily quarantine themselves in their cabins due to suspicion of coronavirus.

"Meanwhile, the United States has seen a dramatic rise in reported cases since the first one back in January. Washington officials are moving slowly as they analyze the situation but have said they believe the USA should be okay."

Geesh. Looks like I'm seriously out of touch, all right. Guess there are some drawbacks to a rustic getaway.

Beau gave her a bold wink when he saw her and hurried off, no doubt to make up for a late start. She didn't see much of him, because he was working on the second floor, preparing the Lodge to deal with whatever resulted from what was quickly developing into a pandemic. Apparently, Skye was much more informed about conditions than she was. Probably because the Lodge was considered an emergency relief center, and the current situation wasn't her first rodeo.

Beau had—obviously—added several other workers to the force, and they were busy connecting the cabins. Eve finally saw him again as daylight leached from the Friday afternoon sky, melting into evening. The sunset lit the sky with flames of orange and red, while thunderclouds made a stunning contrast. She caught up with him at his truck.

He wiped a tired hand over his face. The fatigue showed clearly in his eyes. "I need a break."

Her face flushed when she thought of the ways she'd like to provide one. "I can think of something that might revive you."

"Aw, sweetie, I'm too whipped for that."

She smirked. "That too, but Millie's serving mountain trout tonight, fresh-caught. Want some?"

He grinned, and light danced in his eyes. "That I can handle. Rasslin' a mountain lioness is beyond me right now."

"Too bad. So sad." She sashayed out. "Wash up and join me in the dining room." *Oh well. It's too late for some afternoon delight anyway.*

Over their trout, she regaled him with some other pick-up lines she'd received. "One man said, *Touch me.* I just looked at him. Pardon? He winked, then said, *When you do, I can say I've been touched by an angel.*"

Beau let a belly laugh rip. "That was so lame."

"Tell me about it." She rested her chin on her palm. "Skye mentioned she and Luke planned to celebrate the Quad Squad's third birthday soon. She fears John and Marsha Weathers, the grandparents, might have to stay home because the Boomers are the virus's current target. Something about *social distancing?*"

"Yeah, no gatherings over ten people, and you have to stand six feet apart...Hm, your family is bigger than that. No way can you do it. The only way I can get the work I'm doing done is because y'all haven't opened for the spring season.

And quite frankly, I don't see how you can open with the coronavirus threat and mayor's orders."

"Is there some way you can hook up the family? A video feed or something?"

Beau's forehead lines formed a V. "Y'all have iPhone? Laptop? Tablet? Computer?"

"Pretty sure we all do."

"I can figure sumthin' out. Sunday? That's when the birthday party is?"

Eve nodded.

Beau's brow furrowed in thought. "Yeah…maybe Skype or Zoom…let me think on it. I can make it happen, but the ten-person limit still applies to the festivities."

Eve thought a minute. "That means Skye's family and Storme and Craig and Sunny and Jesse can make it in person. The Weathers need to link up, and well, me."

Beau raised his eyebrows, looking surprised. "Why did you make yourself last on the fam list?"

"I'm their half-sister. We all found out very recently. My mom was—is—what you'd call a *gadabout*. No roots. As I got older, I wanted to uncover my roots. I went online, found a genealogy site, and learned John's my bio-dad. Mom and I paid him a *memorable* visit last season."

Beau looked at her. His eyes had a gentle but probing understanding tucked within those depths. "How so?"

"John had no idea whatsoever about my twin and me. Out of the blue, Mom and I showed up. It nearly gave him cardiac arrest. Their uh, connection—literally—was a spontaneous Woodstock hookup."

"Sounds complicated."

She nodded. "Tell me about it."

The days flew past, and the coronavirus spread like apple

butter among all races, income levels, and borders. Beau decided to use Zoom to keep all generations safe. He'd tested the premise by texting a link to Skye, Storme, and Sunny. In seconds, Eve and the three sisters were able to see each other.

Skye frowned. "I really wanted all of us to gather at the Lodge for the quad's bash. I planned on Eve to be there too, not only for the quads, but also to get to know Dad better."

Eve appreciated the thought. A smile lit her eyes. "Thanks, I was hoping for the same thing, but there's no way we can risk their health. I'll connect with him when we're meant to. On the plus side, I'm getting to know my sisters."

"You didn't miss any quality family time..." Sunny said. "Dad was a big ole pile of—"

Storme frowned as soon as she heard Sunny unload. "Sunny Anne, if I could kick you, I would. What are you tellin' her? Let her see for herself. She'll learn who Dad is *now*. He's trying to make amends like Mom is. Back off."

Sunny looked peeved. "I'm tryin' to prepare her, so she doesn't think he's sumthin' he ain't, and when all is said and done, she didn't miss much."

Skye apologized. "Eve, this family is not The Brady Bunch, that old television sit-com..."

Eve burst into the conversation. "No worries. I've got a lot to learn, and I'll be here until I've got what I'm lookin' for. I think this Zoom thing could work for the party, and you can still hold it at the Lodge. I can link in with your parents, and y'all can attend in person. Dad and Marsha and I will use Zoom. We'll be together and make this work. I think I can get Beau to make a cake for the Quad Squad. Not so sure the bakery is open now. Is birthday cake part of an essential function?"

Sunny pounced. "Whoa. Beau and Eve sittin' in a tree. K-i-s-s-i-n-g..."

"Shut up," Eve said, flushing.

"You shut up. Yahoo! I told y'all. Operation Senior Sex rides again. Look at Eve. She's blushing."

Skye looked both relieved and irritated with Sunny, but she ignored her. "That would be a load off my shoulders, Eve. I already have my hands full. Many of the people who help me with them are over sixty-five. They're from the St. Mary's Altar Society. They can't risk being near us."

Eve's mind raced. "Do you want four cakes? A four-layer cake?"

Storme looked concerned. "Just don't let Mom or Sunny cook."

Eve scratched her head. "Huh?"

Storme explained. "Mom uses cannabis, and Sunny adds Gram's secret ingredient."

Eve laughed. "S'right."

Sunny poked a finger toward Storme. "Very funny, so clever, pun girl."

"You're a pun girl."

"You are."

"Am not."

"Are too."

Skye chuckled. "Just ignore them. They've been doing this for years. I don't care if you bake a sheet cake, a layer cake, or cupcakes. Just thank you!" She blew her a kiss over the cyber-space.

In the background of Skye's image, Eve saw several of the tykes—Nick? Luke?—zoom past the screen followed by a screaming Gabbie, or was it Merry? "I suggest we click off now. Bye."

Since Beau was on standby, he'd heard the conversation. "Looks like I get my cooking *do-over*."

"Yeah, but the Pancake Pantry date still stands. I'll collect on it later."

"You'll have to. It's shut down. The mayors of Pigeon

Forge and Gatlinburg shuttered all non-essential businesses. I don't think they're taking birthday cake orders at Food City. How about we bake on Saturday? I should have some free time then."

Eve nodded. "How about meeting me around noon at the Lodge kitchen?"

"Can do."

Eve could not believe how fast the week flew. She and Beau were ships passing in the night. Beau snatched quick but hot kisses whenever he could, each time left her panting, needing, wanting. On Saturday, she began gathering the bowls, ingredients, and pans necessary for baking. As she assembled them on the kitchen counter, she gave thanks to her sister's plans for the refurbished kitchen. There was plenty of space to work.

In next to no time, she felt what she presumed was Beau behind her. His arms stole around her, and he began by kissing her on the neck. Then he tilted her head back and to the side to kiss her. She decided the kiss was precisely what she needed and how she liked it. His hands began to steal across her breast when she pulled away from him, albeit reluctantly.

"This isn't the time for hanky-panky. We got some serious work to do. We have four birthday cakes to bake."

He turned her body to face him. "Tell me you're not as hungry for this as I am."

His hot breath heated her. As he began to caress and kiss her, she abandoned her protests. "Maybe a quickie? Feels like there's a circus going on in your pants."

"If you insist."

Eve swayed on her feet under the deluge of his body-rocking kisses with plenty of tongue, sucking, and lust. She was wearing a tank dress and little else unless black thongs counted. In a heartbeat, she was wet and panting. It didn't take much to free his pulsing cock from his sweatpants. She had no idea where the condom came from, but it was in place. The next thing she knew, her legs were wrapped around his as he lifted her to him and entered her dripping center.

He perched her on the counter, knocking the flour over and sending the sugar sailing. She heard the carton of eggs fall somewhere.

She was so hot, so very hot. She wanted to whip off her dress. Despite the fact they were alone so far, it didn't mean someone wouldn't want something from the kitchen. Millie had plans with her family, but the twins were unpredictable.

Somehow, Beau managed to push her sundress and nothing bra aside, freeing her breasts. He flicked his tongue over her nipples, causing tiny delicious shivers to race down her spine. She clutched a handful of his hair, raising his kissable to-die-for lips within reach, and kissed the hell out of him. With a groan from her and a grunt from him, they came together. With much heaving and heavy breathing, they finally separated.

Beau looked at the mess surrounding him. "Oops. Wish I could say sorry 'bout that, but it was so wild!"

He thoughtfully handed her a paper towel to help her clean herself.

She threw him a grateful look, tried to look stern, but catching the egg—literally—on his face, she laughed instead. "I think I can salvage enough here to make cupcakes, but that's about it."

He met her laugh with a grin and agreed. "They'll be happy enough. The quads are only three, and I'm sure Skye and Luke would understand." He brushed some flour off her flushed-from-sex cheeks—both sets—ass and face.

She swiped the back of her hand across her sweating forehead, causing the wavy locks to form ringlets. Eve grabbed a broom as Beau took the mop, and they cleaned and sanitized the kitchen. She blushed when she encountered evidence of their torrid sex.

Once again, she gathered the ingredients, exchanging cupcake tins for cake pans. The afternoon sun slanted through the windows, telling her their *quickie* had lasted longer than she'd thought, and the cleaning process took even longer. She assigned him the task of measuring the dry ingredients while she began breaking the eggs into a bowl.

Beau looked at her. "I'm good with eggs too."

She quirked a brow. "Judging from the mess on the floor, I'd say otherwise."

"I can make an egg roll, ya know."

She eyed him with doubt.

"Watch." He took an egg and rolled it to her.

She swatted him on his fine ass and began to laugh.

"I can make a mean banana split, too."

She shot him a wary glance, but not before her gaze took a dive toward his crotch. Caught, she flushed.

He peeled a banana making a show of it *splitting* the skin, broke it, and popped half in his mouth. "See?"

"I can see you're" — she held up the crushed walnuts — "nuts about bananas."

"Looks like I'm not the only nut in the bunch. That last remark qualifies you."

Eve mixed the batter while Beau mashed the bananas into the batter and sprinkled in the nuts.

"I bet the quads will like their third birthday banana nut cupcakes," he teased.

She smiled. "They have no choice, since we demolished the rest of the eggs. All we need to do is bake them and cool them." She set the timer.

He reached out and took her hand, looked into her eyes, and said, "Don't get serious about me. You should see others, too."

Eve doubled over in laughter. Her belly laughs filled the air. "Take this seriously? Are you *serious* about *me* already? Man! That was fast. Being here in Gatlinburg is a temporary gig. I don't do *serious*. Not since my fiancé died in the Gulf War. Serious hurts. And I'm no masochist. All this is Sunny's doing." Having said that, she flounced out the door. "I'm sure you can do a *serious* job cleaning up. Take the cupcakes out when the timer goes off. Be sure to turn the oven off. The fire we ignited in here is enough for one day, I'd say. I'll frost them on my own. As it so happens, I have a date tonight. Buh-bye." She waggled her fingers at him as she left.

Chapter Ten: We are Family

ate? Eve has a date? Tonight? Beau wondered why he was such a dumbass. *How did I manage to shoot myself in the foot so fast? After the wildest sex of my life with a red-hot woman, why did I open my big mouth?* He was not through kicking himself in the butt when the timer went off. Jarred out of his thoughts, he had to google how to tell when cupcakes were done baking. Learning he needed a toothpick to stick in the middle of it, he fished around the kitchen, searching for some. Good thing he had taken the cupcakes out of the oven. They looked golden to him. Inserting the toothpick and finding it clean, he rested them on the marble counter to cool and then cleaned the kitchen, stewing the whole time, wondering who the date was.

Weren't they supposed to practice social distancing because of COVID-19? *Not my problem. Let them get fined for breaking the mayor's shelter in place order. Wasn't that one of the reasons I'm hooking up communications via Zoom here at the Lodge? Baking cupcakes, for gawd's sake?* He didn't have much time to think about it because of the insistent desk bell. Wasn't Eve still around to see what's up with that? Should he take care of it, or just sneak out like a dog with its tail between his legs?

It seemed like the ringing was louder than it should be. *What the hell could be that serious? I'll text Eve to see if she knows.* He walked to the Reception Center and nearly passed out. Eve was already there, and so was a tall drink of water with a four-hundred-dollar haircut with shoes to match. It was Deborah, his ex and their son.

At least he thought it was Jake. It was hard to tell, with the dark purple Mohawk distracting him. That was when he wasn't mentally counting numerous piercings covering his face or the tattoos decorating his arms.

Eve's left eyebrow was raised—never a good sign, he had quickly learned—as she dealt with Deborah. "It appears your *wife* and son were directed here for emergency sheltering. No tourists were supposed to visit the town, but here they are."

"Ex-wife," he muttered.

Eve's face looked like it was frozen in ice-cold permafrost. But she was breathing fire—or was that flame just in her eyes? Eve was the only woman he knew who could blow hot and cold at the same time.

"Whatever," she mumbled.

A firm rapping on the door forced everyone's attention away from the current drama.

A military vehicle parked in front of the Lodge, and army personnel piled out. One soldier stood out from the rest. The military gear included a hat that shielded the face of a five-foot-four officer, who said, "We need to talk."

Beau's voice joined Eve and Deborah's, saying the same thing. The simultaneous echo could have been funny, but there was something about the seriousness of the military presence that was definitely not at all funny.

The officer spoke, "I am Second Lieutenant Winters. By executive order of Governor Lee of the great state of Tennessee, the Sugarlands Lodge will hereby be under quarantine due to the coronavirus. All personnel is to prepare to stay under quarantine here. The Lodge will become the barracks for Emergency Response and Preparedness." The officer finished issuing the command and began to direct army personnel inside.

Chapter Eleven: Alone Again

Eve rose to the occasion to show what the Lodge staff had done to become an emergency relief center, as they had in the past. Meanwhile, she texted Skye.

Help. SOS. Or maybe May Day.

Beau and the others stood there in shocked silence as she prepared to play guide.

Head held high, eyes focused, Eve snapped to attention and led the lieutenant for the Emergency Response Preparedness Team through the Lodge. With a sweep of her hands, she showed them to the Banquet Room. Numerous cots were set up six feet apart to maintain social distancing regulations to accommodate whoever needed to use them.

"From past experience as an emergency relief center, we have these cots and bedding ready as well as the second floor, which has eighteen rooms. We also have a dozen cabins out back that can house the staff. There are family quarters as well, since this is a family-run Lodge. Let me know how I can be of further assistance to you."

The brow of the cap shaded the officer's face. With a nod of the head, the lieutenant turned to what Eve assumed was a private of some sort.

The private checked his clipboard and said, "As Lieutenant Winter's stated, this facility has been designated as a barracks for the National Guard. We are here to provide essential services due to the coronavirus pandemic. I need a list of everyone here — including those who are guests, work here, or are on the premises for any reason. Everyone must fill out these forms listing where you live, where you have been the last twenty-four hours, and who you have been with. Moreover, essential workers, those required to keep this facility open, need to complete an additional form.

"From here on out, you will be considered *occupants,* since you'll be residing herein. You will be appraised of your living quarters upon completion of the form and once we assess the situation. All those who are here now will be under the governor's stay-at-home executive order beginning Monday at eighteen hundred hours. Everyone must wear face masks when out of your quarters to keep y'all and my command unit healthy. Those who come into direct contact with any military personnel must wear these N95 masks, for our protection as well as yours."

Another private began distributing face masks.

"You are welcome to make your own when you are on the grounds, but they must cover your mouth and nose. Avoid touching your face, and stay six feet apart. Wash your hands for twenty seconds with soap and water. Hand sanitizer will be provided, as well. Use it upon entering and leaving, just like doctors do. Take this time to get what you need from your homes. Get clothing, prescriptions, care for children or the elderly, et cetera, until further notice." He handed the forms to Eve.

Eve struggled to keep her jaw closed. She could feel it begin to open in shock. She just knew if Sunny were around, she would have asked her if she was trying *to catch flies.*

A parade of military people filed in, and another private assigned the soldiers to *bunks.* Gear and footlockers poured through the doors with the assortment of military men and women.

Deborah and Jake Jobs looked confused. Deborah's well-manicured and well-maintained hand flew to cover her lips as her forehead wrinkled. Her other hand clutched the shoulder of the purple-haired youth. When the young private pushed a mask at her, she looked as stunned as the rest gathered there.

Jake took it but pulled a black leather mask from his vest and donned it. The skull and crossbones were striking. Eve felt an involuntary shiver steal down her spine.

Beau seemed to be floored by the whole tableaux, too.

Eve was equally shocked and surprised by turn. Her eyes moved to catch his gaze. Seeing him raise his shoulders in a what-the-hell-gesture threw her into gear. "Excuse me, but am I to understand that we will not be serving as a field hospital or residence for displaced *tourists*, but we're becoming a...a...*barracks* for the army?"

The young man spoke, "Roger that. You will accommodate the personnel necessary to handle this mission. We will assist with food, staff, and management duties as we service Townsend, Wears Valley, and Gatlinburg during this pandemic. We will be assisting those civilians until further notice. All that can change as the situation warrants. The mayors of the surrounding towns have likewise issued stay-at-home, also known as *Do Your Part—Stay Apart*, orders." A grimace crossed his face, which showed he agreed with what the newscasters dubbed a sing-songy slogan. He cleared his throat. "The mayors strongly encouraged tourists *not* to come to these areas for Spring Break. The Great Smoky Mountain National Park has been closed, as you no doubt already know."

Eve furrowed her brow. "I see."

Jake stood transfixed in front of a painting. He stared at the rendering of a white stag with a full moon appearing between its antlers, which hung above the imposing river-rock fireplace. "This painting's dope."

Eve thought it was impressive too. It had a haunting, mystical, almost magical hold on the viewer. She turned her attention away and looked at Deborah but addressed the private. *"Some* tourists didn't get the message. What do I do with them?"

"Since I see they are already here with their luggage, you can house them for the duration. After Lieutenant Winters assesses the situation, they'll be assigned quarters."

"Well, everyone, you heard the man. Beau and…uh…family, please fill out the paperwork, get your possessions together, and let's get crackin'."

With Eve's help, the paperwork was distributed, then she went to consult with the commander. When she approached the officer, she quickly noted the familiar set of shoulders. Despite the military stance, she knew she had met this person in a shared past. As she neared, familiar blue eyes flashed, and fingers made a signal that she knew well. It was developed when they were only six years old. Seeing it meant, *play along, be quiet…I will fill you in later.* Eve did as directed, not understanding why, but knowing she'd find out soon enough. Eve gave the lieutenant a wink, which she prayed no one else noticed. No one seemed to since they were standing there frozen like deer in headlights.

In a firm but quiet, no-nonsense tone, the lieutenant asked Eve to secure a quiet, *private* workspace.

Eve opened the door to the office she shared with Skye. "I'm the acting co-COO here. You can use our office."

A light appeared in the lieutenant's eyes, and her tone of voice held a trace of repressed humor. "All right. Ms. co-COO is it, eh? I'll look over these forms and let y'all know where your quarters will be."

Eve just looked at the lieutenant. *What the hell does that mean?* "There are cottages out back, as I mentioned. I occupy Little Miss Muffet's currently. The other cabins have been cleaned and prepared." Thinking fast, she said, "Some occupants may be getting groceries, belongings, or prescriptions."

The lieutenant nodded, looked at the forms the private distributed, and said, "I'll need a list of lodge accommodations and cabins. I need to know how many bedrooms each cabin has, which are efficiencies or suites. I'll let you know if you can continue to stay in whozit's cabin."

"Little Miss Muffet's," Eve muttered. "I can pull that information up easily enough. My half-sister, Storme, has already prepared a spreadsheet you'll find helpful. She prepared a map of the premises for our guests, which I'll also provide."

A smile tugged at the lieutenant's lips. "Half-sister, eh?"

Eve nodded and said, "I'll leave you to it. If you need me…"

"I'm sure I can find you."

Eve left the office and went to the Great Room, where she had completely abandoned Beau, who had his hands full with his family. *Wonder what will happen when they learn Beau and I are seeing each other? I wouldn't want to be in his shoes.* Eve then turned her attention to Beau's family. *It's easier to think of them as Beau's family than it is to think his ex-wife is here.* "Would y'all like some sweet tea? A soft drink?"

Deborah threw her a brittle look and still appeared upset. "Do you have any hard liquor on hand? Kentucky Bourbon?"

Eve winked. "We're in the Great Smoky Mountain National Park—no alcohol can be bought or sold—but I can get some coffee if you'd like." She winked. "I have a little something harder in my cabin." Eve excused herself as she led Deborah and her son toward the comfy rustic armchairs that faced the impressive fireplace. "Make yourself comfortable."

"Beau, you know where the sweet tea and soft drinks are for your son." In passing, she looked at Beau and murmured, "We need to talk. Later."

Deborah's well-shaped brow arched—she'd obviously

overheard Eve.

As soon as Eve left the uniformed and civilian assembly behind her, she took the opportunity to text Skye again. *Send in the Calvary. Get Storme and Sunny to Lodge. Now!* Eve poured two fingers of Tennessee Whiskey into a coffee mug to accommodate Deborah. She paused a moment to reapply lipstick and ran a quick hand through her curls. *Deborah looks cool as a cucumber with her oh-so-precise platinum haircut and her Donna Karan slacks and blazer. Hmm, maybe I should take a swig of moonshine too. Gotta look as good as my competition.* She wrinkled her nose and cringed. *Fat chance.*

On her way back to the Lodge, she saw Sunny and Storme arrive. She intercepted them before they could go inside.

"What gives?" Sunny demanded. "What's with the army out front? There's a gazillion jeeps, trucks, and army stuff."

"Give her a chance to catch her breath," Storme groused. "You'll find out soon enough."

"We have a situation here," Eve began. "We've been declared the barracks for the National Guard who've been activated during the COVID-19 pandemic. We've got to get your parents set up in one of the cabins so we can keep them safe, sound, and protected nearby. The elderly are particularly at risk. I said they're out now but are using The Little Old Woman's Cabin. I planned for you both and your husbands to stay here too. You know, a kind of rally round the flag family thing. This virus is no joke. We need to pull together."

The girls nodded. "I'll make sure they pack clothes and meds," Storme said.

Sunny looked like she was going to complain, but then Storme continued, "Craig and I will take a room in the family quarters, and… Sunny, I know, I know, you and Jesse will want Baby Bears Cabin." Sunny backed down.

Sunny piped in. "Good thing Skye and Luke have moved to Amazing Grace this week. The quads have outgrown the living quarters the park provided. We'll be able to conduct the quad's third birthday party without too much fuss, and everyone will be on hand. I'll take care of Mom and Dad. Operation United Family begins."

Storme groaned. "You and your corny operations."

Sunny glared at her and flipped her locks over her shoulders. "They always work, y'all notice?"

Eve stopped at the kitchen's back door to the Lodge. "When you go inside, be sure you fill out the Occupant Forms where you're staying, so the lieutenant doesn't screw with our living arrangement. Be sure to get the Essential Worker Forms, too—just in case."

In the kitchen, she calmly poured coffee into a mug for Deborah, adding a shot of whiskey. *This should mellow the ice queen out.* After she had given Deborah the coffee and received a frosty *Thank you,* she hurried into the Lodge office to pull up The Occupancy Spreadsheet. Eve added Craig and Storme, Sunny and Jesse, and John and Marsha to the roster. Fortunately, the lieutenant was busy doing lieutenant things and wasn't there to know the difference. Eve's plan seemed to work. It was evident that Sunny and Storme got the required paperwork entered on the computer and submitted as commanded. Fortunately, she could access those files using her phone. *Operation United Family is a go.*

CHAPTER TWELVE: YOU CAN'T ALWAYS GET WHAT YOU WANT

It wasn't that often that Beau found himself at a loss, but he really was in a quandary. *How does one handle an ex and the next? Never had to worry about it before Eve.* Eve's gaze was throwing darts at him, and icicles formed whenever Deborah opened her mouth. *She's been acting like the queen of the establishment, having Eve run after her wants and needs.*

When Eve returned with Deborah's doctored coffee, he knew he'd have to make introductions at the very least. *And how do I do that? What's the protocol for that? Does the first wife get introduced first? Does she have seniority? The older get introduced to the younger? That'll go over great.*

He walked over to Deborah, who had hopefully mellowed, when Eve took the bull by the horns, walked up to his ex with a business-like demeanor.

"We haven't been properly introduced. I'm Eve Windsong, co-COO of the Sugarlands Lodge. Since we aren't officially open for the season yet, let me take this opportunity to welcome you. As you can see, the lieutenant and COVID-19 have other plans. Since we're quarantined to this facility, I have a cottage that your family can use. It's a two-bedroom efficiency. I figured you'd probably want to be away from the fray, so how about you take Jump Over the Moon?"

Deborah drew herself together and stood. "Jump over the moon, eh? I think the one *over the moon* is you — with my husband."

Eve startled at the ferocity in Deborah's tone. Her hands

shook, and the color drained from her face. "Excuse me?"

Deborah's glance was sharp. "Don't think I haven't noticed the sparks flying between you two. If you think for one moment that he has time for an, uh, innkeeper, you are sadly mistaken."

Just then, the silence was broken by the sound of boots hitting the floor. The private with his clipboard had returned, as had the lieutenant.

"I see y'all are ready to settle into your quarters." The lieutenant half-smiled then cleared her throat. "The Baby Bear Cabin is assigned to Jesse and Sunny Days. Craig and Storme Knight will occupy The Three Bears Cabin. John and Marsha Weathers will use Mama Bear Cottage while Deborah and Jake will take Jump Over the Moon cabin with Beau Jobs. Millie and Hank will be assigned to The Bakers Cabin."

Deborah said, "That's fine."

At the same time, Beau said, "We're divorced."

The lieutenant continued rattling off room assignments. Both Eve and Deborah looked mutinous.

The lieutenant paused when the private whispered something to her, then looked back to the group. "Divorced? In that case, Beau Jobs will *Covid-cuff* with Eve, as they say, at Mr. McGregor's."

Eve's face flushed. "But I'm at Little Miss Muffet's. Her countenance had no effect on the lieutenant, despite her glare.

"Not anymore."

Eve scowled. "Covid-cuff?"

The private explained. "Couples who have been dating are coupling up, living together, for the duration of the COVID-19 pandemic."

Beau was pleased with the turn of events.

Deborah seethed. "Cohabitation? With my husband? Our son gets exposed to shacking up?"

The lieutenant spoke in a firm tone. "You and your son are

welcome to use an army tent. They're primitive but comfortable. The two of you can quarter in the Elkmont Campground if you prefer. They have restroom facilities a short walk away. Otherwise, you can still take the cabin while Mr. Jobs Covid-cuffs."

Jake apparently saw his opening. "Can I stay with Dad? It's cold at night."

Eve fumed and appeared ready to protest when the lieutenant noticed and growled. "Ms. Windsong, don't look a gift horse in the mouth. Orders are orders. Desperate times call for desperate measures. The remaining cabins are already occupied by my command staff and myself. I'll be quartered in the Caretaker's Cabin, although I will also require space on the second floor. I am not accustomed to explaining my orders. Refrain from questioning them from here on out. Now, carry on."

"But...but... I'm the COO," Eve blurted. "Besides, we've only been dating a little while..."

Deborah ground out. "Dating, my foot. Any fool can see you're lovers! I see the glances, the excuses to touch. You two may fool Jake here, but not me. Beau Jobs, your family is in tatters, your son's out of control... What kind of example are you setting? Now he has to watch you live together with your—"

Beau stood up so fast he knocked his chair over. "That's enough, Deborah. Stop. Now."

Eve gathered herself together and turned to Sunny. "Mrs. Days, will you escort Mrs. Jobs and Jake to their cabin, please?"

"My pleasure." Sunny led them away.

Drew Sunrise, Beau's business partner, arrived at last with the company van and drove him to his condo in Sevierville to pack his clothes. He left his Cadillac in the garage and drove his Jeep to Walgreen's, where he bought a large package of condoms, then headed back to the Lodge to settle in at Mr. McGregor's Cabin.

He parked his Jeep and went through the front door. He noticed Eve's things in the first bedroom, so he took the unoccupied one. *Not going to be presumptuous and move into Eve's room. That would set a really bad example.* He noticed a coffee maker on the counter with the makings for tea or coffee and prepared a cup using the mountain blend he found. As he drank the coffee, he puttered around and noticed a tent placard on the mantelpiece. He picked it up and read a poem called Mountain Magic.

> *According to words of lore in days of yore,*
> *Those who pass through this cabin door*
> *Will find lasting love evermore.*
> *Tis love y'all find*
> *Of the forever kind*
> *Two hearts resting here, for all time, bind.*
> *So mote it be, as y'all see.*

Beau huffed with a skeptic's smile. *Exactly what I need, more complications. Magic? Love? Bah Humbug. Wonder whether Eve's seen this? Think I'll wander over to the moon cabin to see how my out-of-control son is faring.* Absently his fingers fiddled with his right earlobe, which had once held a stud earring that was a hit with the girls back in the day. He gave a small laugh at the memory. *I went from a dud to a stud with one simple pierced ear. So Jake's wearing a purple Mohawk. May mean nuthin'. Best to check it out. Don't want to overreact. I'm sure Deborah has said plenty about his look already.* Worry nonetheless did take up residence in his gut. *Before attacks, get the facts.*

Beau heard a plunking sound at the nearby prong of the river. He spotted a small rock flying through the air. It didn't take a degree in rocket science to know he had found his son.

Jake was indeed the source of the noise—if that plunk even counted as noise. Beau was surprised he'd heard it over the music of the stream. He picked up a stone and pitched it across a calm pool of relatively undisturbed water. It skipped four times and then made a soft plunk before it sunk.

"Good one!" Jake said when he turned to see who threw the stone. "Yo! Wassup?"

"Not much." Beau relaxed and kept his tone casual. He did need to touch base with his son more frequently. Maybe *he* was a missing piece in Jake's puzzle. "Not much. I moved into Mr. McGregor's. Wanna check it out?"

"Why not? Not that I have anything better to do."

"What? You bring your Xbox?"

Jake grinned. "Yup. Mom wouldn't let me set it up, though. Said since we were roughing it, we should do it right. Whatever that means. All she's doing is complaining. Says she's never had it so primitive. Says Appalachian heritage sucks."

"Your mother actually said *sucks*?"

Jake looked down and mumbled. "Not really. But that's what she meant."

Beau looked at his son, marveling at how he was growing like a weed. All arms, legs, and what was sure to be size eleven feet. "Want me to talk to her about it?"

Jake shuffled his feet and kicked a small rock down the path. "Naw, it'll make things worse. She'll come around. I have to use the internet for schoolwork. Speaking of which, is that flat-screen your work? Hooking up this place? Despite what Mom says, I think this Lodge is *sick*."

Beau cringed upon hearing the words *hook up*. He poked his son. "That was a great pun, what with COVID-19 raging."

Jake gave a half-grin. "I'd have said the Lodge was *dope*, but it didn't work as well."

They reached Mr. McGregor's Cabin, and Jake preceded him inside, glancing around the room. "Now this place is truly rad! Epic fireplace, but not as awesome as the Lodge's. Did you see those carvings? Those giant bears. So realistic."

"The owner's father, John Weathers, did all the carvings, I've heard."

Jake plucked the placard from the mantelpiece and read it. "Whoa Dad! You read this? You're in for some serious shit here. Magic." He waggled his fingers, "Ooh, abracadabra, you are falling in love."

Beau laughed and flexed his muscle. "Better put that back, or the one falling may be you."

"That'd be rad, Dad. Ya see what I did there?" He began to wrestle with Beau, laughing, and finally called *Uncle*. "I'd like to learn to carve like that. Think he used a chain saw?"

There wasn't much else in the cabin to check out. Mr. McGregor's Cabin was a two-bedroom efficiency with no shower or bathtub.

Jake hit the mini fridge and grabbed a pop. "This okay with you?"

Beau nodded his permission. He knew Deborah frowned on soft drinks, but he had a rapport to build. One can of soda wouldn't hurt under the circumstances.

Jake took a sip, then said, "Hey, that chick you're with is scary hot."

Beau shifted uncomfortably. "We're just dating. I told her not to get serious about me."

"That's cold, Dad, especially since you're Covid-cuffs now. Mom sure thinks otherwise. And what about that mountain magic thingy. Is that a curse or a blessing?"

"Old wives' tale, nuthin' more. And by the way, the word *chick* is demeaning. We better get back. It's dusk, and your mother may be worried."

Reluctantly, Jake agreed. "The only thing Mom's worried about is the Spa Haus. Is it open for business?"

Beau looked at his son in amazement. *Nothing escapes this*

kid. He shrugged. "I don't know."

Chapter Thirteen: Don't Wanna Be All by Myself

After dinner, and one heck of a day, Eve longed to use the Spa Haus. The Lodge masseuse wasn't back for the new season. Now with the advent of COVID-19 regulations, who knew when it would be officially open. She longed to soak in the sunken tub or even the hot tub, but she had cupcakes to frost for the next afternoon's third birthday party for Skye and Luke's quadruplets. She smiled as she creamed the butter and added the powdered sugar gradually, getting the perfect sweet consistency she was after.

Skye had told her the girls loved pink and purple, so she planned to swirl both colors onto the cupcakes. The boys were into Spiderman, so she checked Pinterest out and found some clever ways to make Spidey webs for them. The adults would just get vanilla buttercream.

She was humming the classic *All by Myself* melody from Eric Carmen when she discovered she was no longer alone. The lieutenant sauntered in, removed her hat, unbound and shook her curly locks, and gave Eve a crushing hug. Dawn — Second Lieutenant Winters — picked up a spatula, used it as a mic, and joined in the chorus.

Eve turned to her twin sister, dressed in fatigues, and said, "Spill."

Dawn laughed. "What, and ruin the fun?"

Eve chuckled. "Why the secrecy?"

"I had to do what I had to do officially first. Morale, keeping up appearances, be sure the twin thing didn't interfere, and all that yadda, yadda, yadda. Besides, it was fun. You should have seen the look on your face! I shacked you up with your boy toy, didn't I? Some thanks I get. We should be talking about how and why I'm here, ya know."

Eve hooted as she placed the last cupcake beside the others, adding a number three on each of the quads' cupcakes. "We will. First things first. Boy toy? That I can get behind. He just told me not to get serious about him, so that's a perfect description of what he is now."

Dawn's face registered surprise. "He did not!"

"He did."

"The cad."

Eve nodded. "He was the epitome of that old adage *when you find yourself in a hole ya just dug for yourself, stop digging.* But he didn't. He dug himself in deeper."

She took off her *Kiss the Cook* apron and added, "I'll text Sunny and Storme to join us at the fire pit—to talk or bond? It's dark enough now."

"Just as long as we social distance. Six feet away and all that."

Eve nodded. "Can do."

"So I'm gonna get to meet your—our—half-sisters? That'll be a hoot. By the way, why the cupcakes?"

"Skye, the oldest Weathers' girl, had quadruplets three years ago—"

"No way!" Dawn's tone said a mouthful. "Wow. Just wow. Better her than me." She shook her head. "Can I borrow some leggings and a top? I don't have any civvies."

"Just like in the old days. Sure. Just don't wear my electric blue cashmere sweater."

Forty minutes later, sitting the required six feet apart, Eve introduced Dawn—who was wearing the electric blue sweater—to her half-sisters, Storme and Sunny.

She winked at her twin. "I knew you'd make a beeline for that sweater. That was my intention all along."

"Sure it was. Keep tellin' yourself that long enough, and maybe you'll believe it," Dawn teased. "By Gawd. We all *do* look alike! I thought Mom and Eve were pulling my leg. Like I have a father that I can actually meet. And, uh, sisters. We have to be family, after all! Go figure."

Eve grinned. "Told ya so. Poor John. Poor Marsha. It was huge shock. On top of that, John keeled over when he saw me. We all thought he'd had a heart attack. Seems like you and me, Dawn, go back to Woodstock and John Weathers."

Dawn was thoughtful. "Well, we knew about Woodstock, but Mom never said anything about John…"

"Mom got around. Said she didn't know his name, the way I heard it. I used a genealogy kit thing…"

Dawn gave her a wry smile. "Inquiring minds want to know. But wow!" She rubbed her hands together. "Where's the moonshine? Let's get this party started."

They all laughed while Eve filled glasses with what the Weathers girls called *Gran's secret recipe.*

Dawn turned to the half-sisters. "How will I tell you apart?"

"You won't. Unless our husbands are around." Sunny giggled.

Understanding obviously hit Dawn instantly. "You played Dynamic Duo, too?"

Sunny nodded. "We called it Twin Switch."

Storme choked on her moonshine and sputtered. "Too bad you never played by the rules."

"Did too."

"Did not."

Dawn laughed, "Now, I know beyond any doubt we are

sisters! We do that too."

Eve teased. "Do not."

"Do too," Dawn chimed on cue.

"I'll drink to that," Storme said, pouring another round, then looking at Eve. "Was Dawn a pain in the behind?"

"Oh yeah!"

"Tell me about it," Storme said. "For me, it began at birth. She was a pain from minute one."

"What—"

"Shut up," Eve and Storme said together.

"Let me tell you a story…" Storme began. "One day, when we were about four years old, Sunny poked me and took my goldfish snack. I pushed her back and grabbed hers. Sunny pulled my hair. When Mom looked to see what happened. Sunny was comforting *me*, with a hug no less. I pushed her off and then got punished for not *being a good big sister*. I had to sit in the corner. I thought about different ways to throttle her the whole time I was there."

Dawn butted in with a story of her own. "Well, I remember when we were in middle school and went on a shopping trip. While checking out some tops, Eve thought she saw me and called out, *Over here, Dawn,* only to discover she was waving at her own reflection. I saw that and never let her live it down. As this discussion proves."

Eve countered. "You're the mirror image of me."

"Am not."

"Are too."

Eve steamed. "You're just the rough draft."

"No, you are."

Sunny laughed. "If Skye were here now, she'd say, *knock it off.*"

"What I am," Eve thundered, "is God's way of saying *buy one, get one free.*"

Dawn struck back. "At least I didn't forget your birthday!"

Eve dug her heels in. "How could I forget it? We're twins!"

"I rest my case. You have to *say* the words for it to count."

Storme looked at her sisters. "We had hand signals."

"So did we!" Eve said.

They all crossed their fingers. Everyone looked incredulous, because they all used the same hand signal.

"What's yours mean?" Eve asked.

"*You and me. We got this.*" Storme winked at Sunny.

Eve came back with, "Ours means *play along, be quiet, I will fill you in later.*"

Sunny laughed so hard, she choked on her apple moonshine. "I set Craig and Storme up."

Storme reacted like a live wire had gone through her central nervous system. Her arms went out from her sides and froze mid-air. "You so did not! Shut your trap."

Amazingly, Sunny managed to do just that.

"Story! Story!" Dawn chanted. "Spill."

"Once a long, long time ago, Storme caught Craig kissing me behind the Smokehouse—" Sunny began while Storme appeared to struggle not to choke her. Again, Sunny played innocent. "What? I was breaking him in for you. I did you a favor and taught him how to kiss. Plus, I saved your reputation, but do I get any thanks? Noooo."

"It wasn't that long ago."

Then Storme asked, "How did you save my reputation?"

"When he tried giving me tongue, I bit it."

Storme smacked her forehead. "Sunny, I swear, I'll shake you till your teeth rattle!"

Eve smiled. "I can top that one. My boyfriend came to the house to take me out. Dawn came down the stairs. Stu looked at her and smiled. *I like what you've done with your hair.* He kissed her. Dawn kissed him back. Then she called up the stairs, *Eve, your boyfriend's here.* Even worse, I hadn't changed my hair. Dawn had.

"Stu was shocked, but things got worse several months

later when Dawn posed as me and attended the Homecoming with Stu. He got the shock of his life the next day when I slapped him in the face for standing me up. His face went white, and he swore he'd taken me. Even claimed he was innocent and would swear on a stack of Bibles that he took me.

"We both turned to Dawn, who tried to look innocent. I accused her of stealing my boyfriend, but she denied it, saying, *No, I stole your Homecoming date. I brought him back. What's your problem? You could show everyone the pictures. They'd never even know the difference.*"

"That happened to us! I swear to God, word for word! Just change the names to Abe and Sunny. I kid you not. For us it was Prom. God, help us." Storme refilled their mugs with moonshine. "This is the last of the moonshine."

The four sisters howled with laughter.

"Oh. My. God! We are *real* sisters." Dawn cried out.

"Welcome to the family," Storme and Sunny chorused.

"Then, there's the fishing story," Sunny began.

Storme threw Sunny a stormy look.

"Tell us," Dawn said.

Sunny spoke in a rush. "Let's just say Storme caught Craig and leave it at that. I better not open that can of worms."

Sunny leaned over to Storme and whispered, "Should we warn them?"

Storme shrugged. "About the mountain magic?"

Sunny continued. "Yeah. Shouldn't they be prepared?"

"May as well tell."

Eve overheard them. "Tell us what?"

Sunny cleared her throat, "Word has it that the Lodge is full of what's called mountain magic."

Eve looked at Storme and Sunny like their synapses had misfired.

Dawn gaped. "Say what? Magic?"

Storme began where Sunny left off. "Lore has it that two things are operating here at the Lodge. People meet here or stay here and end up falling in love. If they see the Ghost Stag, they're soulmates and will have children pretty quickly. It's said to be quite strong at the Mountain Magic cabin."

Eve sighed in relief that she wasn't staying in that cabin.

Dawn hooted. "Now, I've heard everything. What's with the Ghost Stag?"

Sunny answered. "It's a white stag. Very rare. Probably an albino or something. But Jesse and I saw it. And look. Here we are all married and everything." She showed her ring finger as proof.

Apparently, Dawn wasn't swayed. "I've seen the map. You made it yourself, Sunny. There's no cabin named Mountain Magic on the premises."

"Oh, but there is," Storme injected. "When we three inherited the Lodge, we changed most of the names to nursery rhyme characters, but Mr. Mc Gregor's was the original Mountain Magic cabin."

Eve felt the blood drain from her face.

Sunny laughed. "Some say Poppa used to change the signs on the cabins every now and then whenever he saw a likely couple come his way. He was the original matchmaker. There's even a room called that in the Lodge's main building, but most folks don't know about it."

Dawn's face blanched. "Say what? I have a room there, too. Don't tell me…"

Sunny giggled. "Okay, we won't."

Storme didn't laugh. "Something special happens here, though. The spirit of this place is love. Several couples have married after staying here. Not just me and Sunny but Poppa and Gram, Skye and Luke, and Dr. Cyd and Rod Garden."

Sunny chimed in. "Even our parents have a romantic history in the Weathers Cabin on the far side of the premises."

Eve stood up. "Hogwash. I'm going to bed."

"Just pray you and Beau don't see the Ghost Stag. That'd

be a double whammy," Sunny warned. "Don't say we didn't warn you."

"Bullshit," Dawn announced, putting the dying embers of their fire out.

Spring was in the air, but as the fire died, the mountain air chilled, and Eve shivered. Whether it was due to the legend or the cold, she couldn't say for sure. She had to watch her step on the way back to the cabin. *Dawn's right. What BS.*

Once inside Mr. McGregor's, out of habit, she pulled her top off, along with her hoodie, and did a little dance freeing her legs from her leggings. She balled her clothes and lobbed them toward the bathroom just as Beau emerged. Her clothes hit him squarely in the face.

"Feel free to throw your panties my way. Then bring your sweet self over here, and we can both get naked and — "

Heat flooded Eve's face, and she swore she felt her whole body blush. She had gone braless and stood there in her string bikini panties. *Damn! I forgot about him.* "In your dreams, Mr. Don't-get-serious-about-me. Ta-Ta." She waggled her fingers at him as she sashayed into her bedroom and firmly closed the door.

Chapter Fourteen: Celebrate Good Times

The morning sky was an umbra of pink, blue, and gold, but it was all but lost on Eve, whose head pounded. Nevertheless, daylight peeked through the curtains, insisting that she get up and face the day. Although she slept nude, she remembered Beau was her COVID-19 roommate and pulled on pale gray sweats and hoodie. Bleary-eyed and squinting, she half walked, half stumbled into the living room, where Beau met her with a steaming cup of mountain blend coffee.

She mumbled her thanks. "Why is this morning so loud? Ow, my aching head. I need Millie's Tail of the Dog Ole Mountain Remedy. What day is it?"

Beau chuckled. "It's Sunday, but don't worry about Mass. The services at all the churches 'round here are closed due to the coronavirus."

She bolted upright. "Christ Almighty! It's Sunday? Already? Shit!"

Beau cocked a brow and drawled, "That's some bad Sunday morning talk comin' out of such a pretty mouth. Never heard *Christ* and *shit* in the same sentence before."

If looks could kill, Beau'd be a goner. She glared at him. "I gotta get my act together. Today's the birthday party for The Quad Squad. I have things to do."

"You're fine. Millie heard the ruckus last night and hand-delivered her ole timey hangover remedy to y'all. She made some for your sisters, too. It's in the fridge. Finish your coffee, and I'll get it." He chuckled before adding, "I got a text from Skye, and she has pizza ordered and knows the cupcakes are ready. I've sent the invitation and password for Zoom to all involved, and I conducted a dry run, smoothed out the kinks, and the party's on. Your, uh, other parent finished carving his gifts for the kids, and the gifts are already over there. Chillax, as Jake would say."

Relief coursed through Eve. "Oh."

With each sip of her coffee, her alcohol-induced ire faded. She still felt *off*, but experience had taught her Millie's cure-all would, well, cure all. She tucked her feet under her and listened to the birdsong. She could hear a woodpecker outside and wished it would move on, as the pounding headache seemed to amplify with each peck.

"I guess I don't have all that much to do after all. I'll be a guest, not the host. Phew! I'll be watching from here." Her glance fell on her laptop. "How'd that get here? Are those our cupcakes?"

"Yup. Dawn sent a private over with all that. Your laptop screen will make it easier for you to view the celebration. I agree we did our part bakin' the world's best banana cupcakes. How'd the frosting go?"

"Them's fightin' words, buddy. I did most of the work. You bugged out."

"Hey, I was willing. You got mad at me. So shoot me. I didn't want to lead you on. In my experience, women tend to get serious fast at our age. I meant no offense. I was being upfront with you."

Eve looked at him, dumbstruck, but her ire was still evident in her tone. "As I've *already* said, this is a temporary gig. I'm outta here after I finish what I came here to do. I don't do serious, and I don't date all that much. Talk about keep on digging that hole you're in. Geesh."

He cocked his brow in her direction. "Seriously? You are

sumthin' else, woman."

"Yup, that's what they all say." Then she waltzed over to the kitchenette and retrieved her cure-all cocktail. When she glanced back, she watched him struggle to close his mouth.

"Hey," he called after her, "can we be friends, or shall I say Covid-cuffs with benefits?"

She threw a dishtowel at him. "Maybe. Maybe not."

Eve noticed the Sunday paper on the couch, opened it, and began to read. "This whole paper is filled with nothing but coronavirus info! What the president said, and the World Health Organization's position. Looks to me like this is way more serious than anyone thought. I sure hope the WHO has it right. This is scary. Hell, the frickin' National Guard is next door taking over, for heaven's sake."

"When I was in Walgreen's last night, they had giant X's on the floor at six-foot intervals. I pulled my bandanna up over my nose and mouth." He showed her as he waggled his eyebrows at her.

"You look like a burglar. You're lucky you didn't get arrested," she shot back.

"Wait until you see Sunny's face mask." He burst out laughing. "They don't make personal protection equipment any better than those girls do."

"What'd she do?"

"You have to see it to believe it. Speaking of that, Storme's was...interesting as well. Ask 'em to show you. By the way, are you up for some banana pancakes?"

Eve flushed. She remembered well their very hot, very messy banana kitchen caper.

"What I'd say?"

She swatted at him. "Sure. Make my day."

"So long as you stay out of the kitchen. You make a mess, lady."

Eve stuck her tongue out.

Just before the party started, Eve spotted Sunny, Jesse, Storme, and Craig pulling up to the Lodge. She knew Skye and her family were already there. Luke had come by earlier and picked up the cupcakes.

She queued up on Zoom and saw that everyone wore their face masks. She unmuted her speaker and called, "Hey Sunny. Yoo-hoo, over here. Let me see your mask."

Sunny sat in front of the computer. Her mask said *Eat your heart out, I'm married.* There was a big heart shape for the word *heart.* Eve giggled.

Sunny summoned Storme over. "Take a gander at Storme's."

This time Eve gasped and then drew up the biggest belly laugh she ever produced. "What are those little squiggles? They look like… No! Don't tell me…"

"Yes, ma'am," Storme said, deepening her southern drawl. "Them there are penises. If any of them army guys try to get frisky, I tell 'em, *If you can see these here cockwillies, stand back, you're too close.*" Then she giggled. "I bet the birthday boys will love 'em."

She winked and removed her mask, pocketed it, and substituted one with a leopard print. "This one is kid-friendly."

Eve was sure they would love her mask but was secretly pleased Storme made the switch. "What about Skye?"

"I made one for her. Hers has blue balls on it."

"You did not."

Storme nodded and winked.

The screen began to fill up as the couples and quads filed into the dining room. They arrived like a tornado that hit at night in a rainstorm, you hear it before you see it, but it strikes at a furious clip. The quads wore facemasks as well. The girls had purple and pink pooh emoji's and the boys had brown poop masks. Eve cracked up.

"You are a poopy face," Luke told Gabe, who repeated it to Merry, who told Gabbie.

The quads all bounced around laughing as if it was the funniest thing they'd ever heard. They laughed so hard they fell to the floor and rolled over each other like a litter of roly-poly puppies.

Storme giggled when she saw the tykes. "Skye really knows her kids."

"She's a saint," Eve muttered, noticing the kids were now chattering about the army.

"Where tanks?" Luke asked.

She shook her head and smiled. She didn't feel the pang she'd once felt when seeing young children. A wise woman once told her, *If ya don't have 'em to laugh over, ya don't have 'em to cry over either.*

John and Marsha joined them on Zoom from their cabin, and their faces filled their spot on the screen. High pitched cries of *Pawpaw John* and *Memaw Marsha* worsened Eve's headache. There was no keeping six feet apart with the children all over the place, but with only ten people in total, they were in compliance with the state mandate. No doubt Dawn, as Second Lieutenant Winters, wouldn't take kindly to any infraction on her watch.

Gifts were exchanged and cellphone cameras caught precious memories while Eve heard coughing in the background.

Marsha pounded John on the back, concern lined her face. "Keep the party going. I'll give him some of my Tennessee Whiskey, wild cherry n honey to ease his cough."

"I'm fine. I'm—" John's loud cough interrupted his claim. His screen image faded.

"Pawpaw went bye-bye," Merry noticed. "Come back, Pawpaw. We have Spidey cakes to eat."

Luke quickly picked her up and held her upside down. It worked. That quick move distracted her. He picked Gabbie up as well, roaring like a Spidey beastie.

Squeals of joy pierced everyone's ears while Eve began to feel a tingling tickle in her throat. *This is some helluva hangover.* But she didn't let it bother her. *I'm fine. It's just a hangover and being chilled from last night's outing.*

Eve cringed and turned the sound down. *Reminder to self. Never fret about not having kids again.*

Finally, John's coughing subsided, and he and Marsha were back on Zoom. He was just in time to watch the quads open their hand-carved hobby horses that he'd made. The girls' hobby horses had purple and pink manes while the boys' had brown, and each had the child's name carved into the bodies. The quads squealed and were off and riding.

A short time later, the boys, Luke and Nick, produced toy guns, and the bedlam didn't cease until the pizza was gobbled and shouts of *Spideyman* filled the air. The *Happy Birthday* song rang out, and the quads blew out their candles. Soon frosting smeared all four tiny faces.

"This is why I don't have kids," Eve muttered.

Jake showed up to watch the festivities, too. He sat away from his Dad and Eve, maintaining the social distance rule. Beau officially introduced them.

Jake rose and said, "I'd shake your hand, but we can't do that anymore." He gave her an elbow bump instead, and they shared a laugh.

Eve noted he was wearing a black leather face mask with a skull on it. She made a note to herself to bring his good manners and compliance to Beau's attention. If Jake was so *out of control*, would he readily comply with the orders? His manners were definitely in order, as well as a good sense of humor. She found herself liking him.

CHAPTER FIFTEEN: SO HAPPY TOGETHER

Eve exited Zoom and moved her laptop to the coffee table. She curled up beneath the quilt that stretched across the back of the couch. She had to admit the past two days had been quite demanding and draining. Her headache hadn't really improved, and she felt whipped. For the first time in a long while, she felt like taking a late afternoon nap. She glanced around for Beau but didn't see him. *He must be checking on Jake or working on their communications issues. No matter. Not my job to keep track of him. Too bad, so sad. Maybe we could have had make-up sex. Gawd! I must be tired, what am I thinking?*

Before drifting off to sleep, she thought of how she enjoyed being on her own. She liked answering to no one, doing what she wanted, when she wanted. *My life's good. So why was I looking for Beau? I shouldn't care where he is or what he's doing. Right? I don't need the pain or the gain of having a man around restricting my life or my time.*

Beau was feeling rather proud of himself. *That Zoom party went damn well, if I do say so myself. If I were a peacock, I'd display my feathers. My system worked. The family enjoyed their connection. Think I'll check on Jake and the rest, then I'll use that shower shed Deborah talked about. I'll social distance, even though most everyone is gone now — if you don't count the National Guard.*

He wracked his brains but couldn't recall any specific directives saying the shower place was off-limits. He headed for the Lodge to check that all the equipment was in order. In his bedroom, he packed his duffle bag, donned his bandanna, and wore his knit gloves once he got to the door.

He found Jake transfixed before a breathtaking painting. Storme was behind the counter and fortunately had a much less provocative mask on this time. God only knew what Jake would have made of the other. This face mask was color coordinated, matching her blue eyes beautifully. She joined Jake and Beau in the Great Room.

She walked over and stood beside them. "I see you like the art we've commissioned."

"It's totally rad," Jake said.

Storme looked at him. "A local artist, CeCe MacDonald, painted that in my Gram's memory. CeCe has a shop on Glades Drive near my dad's, out in the artisan's Great Smoky Arts and Crafts Community Center. You'd enjoy going there. Too bad we have a mandatory stay-at-home order. I probably can't introduce you to her now, but maybe someday. Do you know the story behind the painting's subject, The Ghost Stag?"

A spark glowed in Jake's eyes. "A story?"

"A mountain myth, some say. Nonetheless..."

Beau looked at the painting and noticed that Storme watched him closely as she spoke.

"They say there's magic in this Lodge. Goes way back to the Cherokee legend, and something similar is mentioned in Celtic lore, too. The Ghost Stag is always white. That's the ghost part."

Jake's eyes lit with recognition. "Kinda like Casper the Friendly Ghost in old-time cartoons?"

Storme looked at him with admiration in her eyes. "You know your cartoons? That one's way before your time."

"We have some electives at school. I'm taking a historical look at mass media entertainment. It includes some way old Mickey Mouse, Popeye, Looney Tunes, and others. Hence

Casper."

Beau did a mental double-take. *Who knew?* "*I'm* a classic film buff, son."

Jake's brow lifted in surprise. "Epic! Maybe we can catch some old classic flicks while we're here. But Storme, stick around, please. Tell me the legend."

Storme was happy to comply. A knowing smile crossed her face. "If lovers spot the stag, it's because only true soulmates can see it. Then they feel compelled to be together no matter the cost."

"Yeah, there's something in Dad's cottage that talks about everlasting love. Is this part of the local legend?"

"If my Gram were here, she'd tell you her love story was no legend. It was as real as we are. Mountain magic, she called it. My folks definitely are proof of the power of enduring love and the hold this mountain has on people. It gets in your blood. It's downright magical when you experience it. Just letting the love in. By the way, my dad carves Ghost Stags of all sizes." With a wave of her hand, she indicated the carvings strewn throughout the Lodge. "In the recent past, Sunny and Jesse saw the Ghost Stag, and guess what?"

"They're married."

Beau shifted on his feet, uncomfortable with the talk.

"Dad's staying in the Mountain Magic cabin, isn't he?"

Beau grumbled and made the correction. "Mr. McGregor's Cabin. Baloney. No disrespect, mind you, but that's just pure myth. Nuthin' to it."

Storme shook a warning finger his way. "Call it what you will. Doesn't mean it's not true. Many things you can't see are real. And Eve is quite a catch."

Beau harrumphed and pretended to clear his throat as he choked down a laugh. "Eve and me? She thinks hugging me is like hugging a porcupine."

Storme looked thoughtful. "Hmm, she let you that close,

eh? That's progress, I'd say."

Jake looked at his father. "It's probably your corona stubble, Dad. Or is that scrub brush on your mug a sorry excuse for a beard?"

Beau laughed and decided to leave before the list of his grooming grew any larger. *Maybe I should shower and shave.* He headed for the cabin. The couch was empty, the quilt spilled onto the floor, and Eve's door was closed. He grabbed his gym bag, making sure it held fresh clothes. He also took his shaving kit and checked it to see if the condoms were inside. *Never hurts to be prepared.* He pulled up his bandanna facemask more securely and left the room with an *adios amigo* salute.

Eve awoke but didn't feel any better. On the contrary, she felt cold. Like she was developing a cold. She decided a full immersion in the Spa Haus hot tub might cure what ailed her. She found her fleece PJs and stuffed them in her tote bag. She grabbed a face mask that wasn't fancy, fetching, or stylish, but it was serviceable.

She had her gloves, hoodie, and face mask on. She doubted that Dawn would let the troops or whatever they were called use the Spa Haus, but no one had told her she couldn't. *If my sister gives me grief, I'll tell her it's therapeutic.* She shed her clothes and mask after leaving her tote bag in a small dressing room. She grabbed the water-repellant U-shaped neck brace and slid into the steaming tub. Her whole body ached, and the water felt so good. She swore her very bones hurt. How could bones hurt? Joints could ache, especially bone on bone, but she didn't have that problem. Yet it was hard to argue with her body. A soothing eucalyptus mist was available with a simple touch on the pad. The mist should help the slight cough she'd developed. She sank beneath the jets and was surprised when a body bumped hers.

She sat up and knocked the neck pillow into the churning hot water. "What the hell!"

"Chill. I didn't mean to startle you, but I saw you here. I might have saved your life. I think you need mouth-to-mouth resuscitation. May I?"

"I may have a cold coming on..." She giggled and forgot she was PO'ed with him. "If it's a matter of life and—"

Beau didn't hesitate. He gave her the full-on Monty and kissed her until she was limp.

He, however, was anything but limp. His lips traced the line of her jaw to her ear lobes. Sensations of delight lit her from within and without.

She wanted him. She ached for him. She grabbed his rod, which was hard and almost ready for her.

He pulled her onto his lap and kissed her some more. His hands cupped and then caressed her breasts. He lifted one toward the jets and then lifted her above him, so the jets hit her sex.

Her climax was swift and fierce—but also sweet-oh-so sweet.

He eased her down onto the seat beside him.

Eve purred. "Mm, that was nice. Too bad we have no protection..."

He untwined from her and said, "Oh, but there is." He knelt, water dripping down the wall of his ripped chest and washboard abs. He stretched his arm, reached over the edge of the hot tub to snatch a foil package, and held it up. "Always be prepared, remember? And this one's lubricated. Ya know, so it will go on wet skin easily."

"What a boy scout." She groaned with a huge grin.

He waggled his eyebrows as he ripped the foil open with his teeth.

"My hero," she said in a husky, low tone.

Her tone changed once he caught a nipple and played with it until he had her panting with desire, ready for some hot action.

"Yippie!" she said as she helped him ease the lubricated condom across his pulsing, rock hard cock.

He guided himself into her as he pulled her toward him, her ass resting on his knees. His hands caressed her clit and labia as he began to thrust. "Never get mad at me again."

"Don't say anything stupid again, and you won't have to worry about it."

He eased himself out of her and playfully smacked her ass. "I could make you regret that remark. Make-up sex has something about it that's unlike any other kind."

"Prove it."

He grinned and pumped into her, thrusting deep.

To prevent him from saying something stupid, she quickly occupied his mouth with a kiss that was designed to make him feel it from his nose to his toes. She came hard for the second...or was it the third time?

He stared at her and said, "Maybe we should always have sex here."

"Why?"

"That way we can avoid the curse of the cabin."

"What curse?"

"The soulmate curse thingy."

She gazed back, caught off-guard. "Some'd say it was a blessing, not a curse."

He winked. "Sounds serious to me."

It was her turn to stare. "Maybe serious is okay sometimes."

Beau grinned. "Methinks I was wrong about the word *serious*. Under certain conditions, it's probably ideal."

"Is that your way of saying, *with the right person?*"

"Yeah, don't get serious about me admitting I'm wrong."

Eve threw him a small smile. "Was that a caveman apology?"

He caught her close to him and kissed her thoroughly. His hands wandered over her body, caressing it.

She playfully brushed him off. "Even real he-man cavemen can't recover that fast."

"Wanna bet?" He chuckled but got out and extended a hand to her.

Eve thought she should take a shower, but she was pleasantly exhausted. She wrapped herself in a bath sheet, found her soft fleece PJs, and cocooned herself within. The top had a wonderful hood. She slipped on suede moccasins and headed back to the cabin.

Dusk fell as she carefully wound her way through the maze of trees while the moon slowly rose and mountain mist rolled in. What she saw next had her frozen in her tracks. She stopped so suddenly Beau ran into her.

"Wha —" he started.

She turned quickly and put a finger to his lips.

Together, they watched the snow-white fur emerging from the mist. An eight-point rack deer stood tall, and damned if it didn't just stand there staring right through them. It did not bolt and run. It stood there regally.

Eve felt the air leave her lungs in a long stream. The Ghost Stag, slow as a sloth, crossed their path, looked back at them, and then ambled away as if to say *Silly humans. What will be, will be.*

"Son of a bitch!" Beau and Eve said together and just stared at each other.

Beau nudged Eve along the way without another word. Once inside the cabin, he went straight to the fireplace and built a fire. They ate the dinner Millie had left inside on the counter. Eve had little appetite, though. They had seen the Ghost Stag. They were in Mountain Magic cabin, *Covid-cuffing*, for Pete's sake, and they were definitely lovers. *I should be ravenous, but I'm not. Beau must have satisfied both appetites.*

Eve snuggled with Beau on the couch, and Beau covered her with a quilt. She fell asleep to the sound of his steady heartbeat.

The next morning, when Beau made coffee, Eve had no desire to drink. If she hadn't seen him drinking some, she wouldn't have even noticed. She simply didn't smell it. Nor did she want anything to eat. She felt like she had a cold and hoped she hadn't given him one, too. *It'll be hard enough living with someone without a head cold.*

Eve texted Storme and asked her to take over for her. Since the National Guard had come in, there really was little call for Eve to do much of anything. The Lodge was not open for business. They had been in the process of opening for the season, but the Government had put the kibosh to that. There was now a small military squad doing everything, including KP duty.

The platoon managed food and medical supplies to the area. As a result, the army deemed them essential to their operations and — with Millie supervising — fed them, too. Millie had forged some sort of strategy to let the army *help* her, but she clearly ruled the roost. So far as Eve knew, Dawn had wisely not micromanaged that arrangement.

Eve saw no particular reason to get dressed. She had zero energy, yet she noticed Beau had plucked a jigsaw puzzle from the stash Sunny had equipped each cabin with, and every now and again, she'd add a piece. They weren't exactly doing the puzzle together, but she was glad he had found something to occupy himself with.

As she fiddled, she pondered awhile, then ventured to say, "Ya know, Jake's done quite well with all these new rules. If he were a handful, wouldn't he be fighting all these restrictions?"

Beau looked thoughtful. "Maybe Deborah's catching all the

flak. Who knows for sure if he's complying?"

"He wore a face mask. Many kids his age wouldn't. They tend to think they're naturally immune from life's issues. You know the drill. *Can't happen to me, I'm young.*"

Beau laughed. He flexed his muscles and beat his chest. "Kids. They're into the *what-me-worry? I'm-bullet-proof.* Good point."

"Hmm… And he's interested in the quads, my father's carvings, and even art. He's not causing trouble, from what I see."

Beau smiled. "How do you account for his hair and, uh, body art?"

"New hair colors are trending. Plenty of adults have purple and pink or neon yellow hair nowadays." Eve grew thoughtful. "Ever ask him about it?"

"Naw. I hoped it was a phase and he'd grow out of it, or it'd go out of style. I could live without the piercings, truth be told."

Eve considered options as she placed another puzzle piece in the border. "Maybe you could introduce him to fishing in the stream out back. Get him to open up. Or take a hike."

"Are you trying to tell me something, woman?"

She giggled. "I'm not telling you to take a hike, nada. I'm merely suggesting it for Jake's sake."

Beau relaxed. "You know anything about fishing?"

Eve laughed, "No, but I heard Storme and Craig do. Maybe you three men can social distance and fly fish. The Lodge has fishing equipment, and Luke Scraper is a ranger and can help with permits and tips."

"That's Skye's husband?"

"Yup."

Beau frowned at her as she pulled on fuzzy socks. "Are you cold? Shall I make a fire?"

She nodded. After he lit the fire, he went off to find Luke

and check on Jake in the process. She continued to work on the puzzle.

CHAPTER SIXTEEN: LOVE ISN'T ALWAYS ON TIME

Beau had to admit that maybe just maybe he *should* get serious about Eve, after all. She was proving to be a real asset to him and his family. She'd managed to shut Deborah up and saw things in Jake that he had not. *Hell, I'm noticing a lot I like about her. She's sexy as sin. Hot. Kind. Has a great heart. Wonderfully responsive body, and she likes me.*

As he walked beside the rocky river, he saw the silver back of a fish glinting in the sunlight. He headed toward Jump Over the Moon cabin and found Jake outside fiddling with a downed stick. It looked like he had a knife in his hand. "Whatcha doin'?"

"Whittling, or trying to."

Beau looked on with approval. "You still in Scouting?"

Jake nodded.

Beau beamed. "You already know I was a scout. Maybe if we put our heads together, we can figure it out." His eyes darted around until he spied another decent looking piece of wood. He, too, began stripping it. They both wore their facemasks and stayed the mandatory six feet apart. "How's it going with Mom?"

"Mom's Mom. You know how she is. She's watching *The Bachelor* on TV, so I can't use my X box. Thought I'd get some air."

"Me, too."

Jake grinned. "So, Eve's watching *The Bachelor*, too? You

95

bored?"

Beau laughed. "She's doing a puzzle."

"That's a far cry from the crap Mom's watching."

Beau cocked a brow at him. "Different strokes for different folks. I wanted to see if you were up for some fly fishing?"

Jake smiled. "I could get into it. Two things, though."

"What?"

"We either eat 'em or release 'em."

"Deal." Beau extended his hands. "Shake on it."

"No way. I'm no Covidiot. Elbow bump."

Beau let out a huge belly laugh that doubled him over.

Jake laughed as well. "I want to learn carving from Mr. Weathers somehow. I've looked at some podcasts on my phone to get some tips."

"Maybe John has a podcast. He has a smartphone, so maybe he's turned to technology, since we're essentially on near lockdown. Other craftspeople must be facing similar issues. Check it out. Maybe Eve has his number."

Beau looked at his son, and for a moment, saw him without the tattoos and piercings. In his mind's eye, he saw another boy, a duplicate. *Kyle. Jake's twin brother, who died of cardiac arrest — gone in an instant.* He closed his eyes against the pain. "You feel him, son?"

"Huh?"

"Kyle. Can you imagine him in this setting?"

Jake froze. His hand began to shake, and he nicked himself. A droplet of blood fell on the wood, staining it. "Why'd you bring Kyle into this? Do you wish he were here and not me?"

It was Beau's turn to freeze. Stillness stole through the woods on silent feet. *Breathe. Just breathe.* "It's okay to think of Kyle. To say his name."

Jake's shoulders began to shake. "Stop. Just stop talking about him. You're the one who can't stop thinking and talking about him. That's what broke you and Mom up. Kyle's death.

My reaction to it. Everything's Kyle. I'm sick of the Kyle drama. Yeah, I miss him. Hell, yes, I feel him, every minute of every single day."

Beau looked at him. "Me too." He said it quietly, but it rang out in the air reverberating through the hills, like an empty echo.

"I thought if I wore my hair like this, maybe you'd see *me* when you look at me, not my brother. All I do is remind everyone of him. But no. You see me and automatically think of him. I see you bleed every time you look at me." Jake threw the wood down, sucked on his wounded finger, and stalked off.

Well, that bonding time just went to hell in a handbasket. What Jake said was true. Too true. He missed Kyle. The brothers were identical twins, but that was where the similarity had ended. They were very different people. *Kyle was athletic and outgoing. The brothers were the yin and the yang, not only for themselves but for us. That's why the hair, the piercings. It had begun before Kyle died. Jake's attempt to be pure Jake.* Beau walked back, letting Jake's words claim him. There was a picnic table nearby. He sat and listened to the woodland birds and sounds of the forest, and he prayed. For his son. His family. He hoped the mountain magic would wind its way into Jake's heart to heal him. To heal them all. Slowly Beau walked back to the cabin, still thinking heavy thoughts. *Kyle didn't break Deborah and me up. I did that.* We *broke us up.* He looked forward to seeing Eve.

By late afternoon, Eve felt better than she had in a long time. *That headache was a bitch.* She looked for a distraction and found a Cosmo magazine. It contained a retro idea for how to surprise your man with a blast from the past. Women of the 1950s were advised to spiff up their sex lives by wrapping themselves in saran wrap to greet their mate at the door. Eve thought for a moment. *Even I can be more current than that. Why didn't the men wrap themselves in plastic wrap? Why did the women have to do everything? What let men off the romantic hook? Shouldn't they work at keeping the juices flowing?*

Eve found her face mask and gloves and donned them after doffing all her clothes. She put on her favorite Barry White playlist and grabbed a foil packet to dangle from her fingers. Fingers that itched to run through his hair, trace the V of his pelvic bones, and fondle his balls. She dreamed about a dozen or so different ways to make hot, wet love with him. She eyed a chair and speculated on how best to straddle him. Tie him up for fun? Handcuff him? Blindfold him?

Her glance fell on the quilt that she could lay him down on to have her way with him in every conceivable position she could dream of. She wondered if she could push him up against the wall and kiss her way down his to-die-for body. Maybe they could stand so she could wrap her legs around his firm, tall torso. Her center began to moisten as her daydream continued spinning from one delight to the next, each hotter than the preceding one.

She closed her eyes, savoring the sensations yet to come. She heard the door open, followed by a gasp. Felt the shivers of desire race through her. Waited for the warmth of his touch. Yearned to taste his sweet, warm mouth. "Wanna play doctor? Perhaps you should get your handsome self over here to examine me."

Sensational thoughts led to torrid desires. All of Eve's senses were engaged. She inhaled and smelled...pot roast? She opened an eye to see a private delivering their dinner! She let out a screech and hightailed it into the bathroom. *Good grief.*

She heard Beau's raised voice. "What's going on?"

The young male private stammered. "She wants a doctor. I wish I was one, but I'm on KP, not a doctor." He paused. "Are you?"

Beau chuckled. "Hardly."

The private shifted on his feet. "I think I'll change my major to go into women's health." He moved further into the room. "I'll, uh, just leave your diner here, okay?"

Beau grunted.

The front door closed, then the music on the cellphone stopped. Then a knock on the bathroom door. She cracked it open to find Beau with her PJs, dangling in his hand.

"That was a major buzz kill," she muttered as she dressed. Her skin was flushed. She hoped she didn't break out in hives due to the epic stress she felt when her plan failed.

Beau rubbed his hands together. "Wash up. Let's eat. We've got tonight." He winked.

They ate and then did the dishes together. When the kitchen was set, Eve turned the TV on. She preferred to watch *My 600-Lb Life*. Beau liked *Dateline*. He pulled out a coin, flipped it and called *tails*...and lost. As they watched, he didn't make one nasty remark. He genuinely rooted for Amanda, who started out strong, cooking good food, eating clean, and even started walking to lose weight. A fight with her enabling mother sent her on a binge eating fest.

Beau was sympathetic. "With that kind of sabotage going on, no wonder she eats."

By the end of the show, Beau said, "I'm hooked. Can we pull up the preceding episodes? This kind of reality television just sucks you right in. I can't believe I never watched this show before. Aren't you happy I installed On Demand?"

She playfully socked him in the arm.

Chapter Seventeen: We Got To-night

The night wore on, and Eve lost track of time. However, Beau was true to his words as he turned off the TV and began to turn her on.

Eve batted her eyes at him. "What's going on?"

"It's night, and that soldier interrupted your plans. So...I'm making good on them."

She smiled when she detected evidence of his arousal. "I can see there's a circus going on in your pants again. I always wanted to join the circus when I was a little girl."

"Hush, now. Let me check you out." He felt her forehead. "I think you may have a fever." He removed her PJ top while feeling every inch of her, beginning with her lips. He traced them lightly with his index finger. "Ouch! Yep. Hot to the touch. I need to listen to your heart." His lips scorched her skin as he made his way down to her *heart...*

"*That*, Dr. Jobs, is not my heart. It's my *boob*."

"Really? Who's the doctor here?" He kissed her long and deep. His tongue plundered her mouth. His hands flowed slowly over her hardened nipples, then continued moving lower. "Hmm, what do we have here? I think I need to examine your abdomen—just in case..." His hand resumed its downward movement. "I need to check you out. I think you sprang a leak." He pushed her PJ bottoms down and off her.

"What kind of doctor are you anyway. That is *not* my abdomen." She giggled. "Obviously, you sucked at Anatomy."

"That may be. Nothing like hands-on learning, though. I can feel your pulse is racing, and your temperature has more degrees than any thermometer. I need to take an internal assessment with my specially calibrated equipment. I'll just insert it to see. Now, where was I? Oh yes, I remember." Expertly, Beau doffed his clothes and pulled a condom from his pocket to sheath himself.

He entered her dripping sex. "Just as I suspected. You do have a very high temperature. Fortunately, I know how to bring your temp down."

Eve cocked a brow. "Do tell." She welcomed him with a warm gush from her core. Her reaction to him was like reaching an oasis after a long, arduous walk through the hot, arid desert.

He lowered his head to pay homage to her needy nipples with his mouth. His hands, feather-light, caressed her breasts. Then he pulled out of her. His tongue circled lazily around her belly button. She bucked.

He moved back up to kiss her lips, nearly drinking what little liquid she had left in her mouth.

She shivered, craving relief, and tried to pull back, to no avail.

His mouth mounted a serious campaign to render her breathless.

Eve pounded on his chest, begging for him to stop the torture to reenter her straining, wanting, hot—oh, so very hot—body.

His kisses made her want more, much more. His caresses caused goosebumps along her skin, which likewise seemed to send strong desire racing through her hot core. Heat gathered between her legs, and her breath quickly turned into panting. She was afraid she'd burst into flames.

"Lady, you are red-hot. You're a furnace melting my dick."

"What can I do?"

"I'll show you." He flipped her over and rained tiny kisses down her spine, leaving her a hot mess.

She pulled a low groan from him when she got hold of his balls. Soon he was the one panting.

Her hands clenched, and her heart rocketed as heat curled in her liquid center.

He entered her and began to inch by wet inch his way into her clenching depths.

Her muscles seized and squeezed him, refusing to let him go.

Nonetheless, he persisted and wriggled himself still deeper, slowly, very, very slowly. Then in a heartbeat, he pulled back, raised her to his knees, and drove into her. He was in so deep she could feel his balls spanking her labia.

Once again, he flipped her until she was on her back and plunged back in, increasing his speed.

Her fingers reached for him, feeling the hairs on his sculpted chest.

His heart thumped fast beneath her touch. His cock was like a jackhammer, slamming into her delighted core. In one last heave, he sent them skyrocketing into a world of sensation and delight as they climaxed. He collapsed on her and drew her close to his chest.

She felt like she was on fire. Not with naked need, and not from lovemaking. She fell asleep on the couch, wrapped in his arms.

Beau worried the next morning when Eve literally felt hot to the touch. He tried to rouse her but had a difficult time waking her up. "You might really be coming down with something. Let's get you in your bed."

Once he had her settled, he coaxed her to drink. "You need fluids. I'll keep a bottle of water on the bed stand. Try to drink it. I'm going to the Lodge to see if I can get a real thermometer. Let's get you into PJs, so you can sweat it out."

When he arrived at the Lodge, he noticed a mother bear and three cubs inside an army truck. One cub was actually at the wheel. He gave them a wide berth, nonchalantly walking as far from them as he could.

He made it inside, spied Dawn, and said, "Those are some bear-y special new recruits out there in your vehicle."

"What recruits? I'm not expecting any. The pandemic shut down any recruiting."

"Well, they're here. Check them out." He led her to the window and parted the curtain.

Dawn's jaw dropped at the sight. "What the fuck! How'd they get in there?"

"Was the truck locked?"

"How the hell would I know? Usually, they're ready to go at a moment's notice."

"These bears can get in unlocked vehicles. That's a mother with three cubs. Better wait until they decide to leave. Never get between a mother and her cubs. Best leave them be."

Dawn let fly an expletive.

Beau continued to worry about Eve as he stared at the bears.

"Why are you still here?" Dawn asked.

"I'm not going out there until that bear leaves." He looked at her like she'd just got off a turnip truck. "I think Eve's got a fever, and I need a thermometer."

"Jesus! Her, uh, our father has a fever, too. I hope we're not facing a coronavirus outbreak here. Two of my squad are isolated already. If she's sick, you'll have to move out. She needs to go into isolation."

Beau felt the blood drain from his face.

Dawn handed him a digital thermometer. "Scan this over

her forehead. Let me know if she's over one hundred degrees."

"If she is, what does that mean?"

Dawn looked concerned. "Trouble. It means trouble. My unit is assembling testing materials. If need be, we'll test her. Any other symptoms?"

Beau frowned in thought. "Other than not swooning at my to-die-for banana pancakes and literally not smelling the coffee, none that I can see."

"Is she having trouble breathing? Any coughing?"

"None."

Dawn nodded. "Could be a cold or flu. Keep an eye on her. If she gets worse, we'll test for coronavirus, isolate, and treat her here. God willing, we won't have to ship her to Mountain Heritage Hospital. We may have to set up as a field hospital after all."

Beau made a beeline for the cabin, dread in his gut. *Dear God, what if she has the coronavirus?* His heart twisted.

CHAPTER EIGHTEEN: RAINDROPS KEEP FALLING ON MY HEAD

"Where's my sister?" Lieutenant Dawn Winters demanded.

It had been two days since Beau had come to the Lodge looking for a thermometer, and Dawn couldn't help but worry.

Beau's brow furrowed. "She's at Mr. McGregor's Cabin. I think she needs a doctor."

Dawn tried to look concerned and coolly professional at the same time. "She'll have to settle for a nurse."

Just like Eve. Man, my sister is the only woman I know who can blow hot and cold at the same time.

She strode to the door and snatched a digital handheld thermometer as she walked out of the Lodge. The day before, they'd quickly set up a field hospital for those not needing ventilators. Dawn worried they might need them and had put in a request for two at least.

Beau looked around. "Where's the nurse?"

Dawn threw him a look that could scorch like an iron on a white shirt. "By profession, I am a registered nurse, and as such, the best we have to offer her right now."

Beau looked surprised.

Dawn kept walking. "Some National Guards enlist after a four-year degree, and some use Guard Benefits to get one. I'm one of those. I know what I'm doing."

Beau had the decency to appear properly chastised and impressed simultaneously.

Before Dawn entered the cabin, she automatically adjusted her N95 facemask. She noticed Beau fiddled with his as well.

Eve was shaking under the blankets. She struggled to breathe and looked flushed.

The lieutenant part of Dawn was brisk, but the sister part donned gloves and felt Eve's forehead. "Hot to the touch," she muttered. She held the thermometer to Eve's forehead. The digital display read 101 degrees. She withdrew some Tylenol from her pocket and handed them to Eve.

Beau pushed a bottle of water into Eve's hand.

Eve's hand trembled, and she spilled some as she tried to drink to swallow the tablet.

Dawn worked to stay cool as a cucumber as she ground out an order. "Beau, get out of here. She's in isolation as of now, and so are you. Go wait outside but don't go anywhere. I'll escort you to the Lodge for a COVID-19 test. Understood?"

"Copy that," Beau said in a meek tone. "Please don't put me in with Deborah and Jake."

Dawn rolled her eyes. She turned to her sister, checking her pulse and assessing her overall state. "I don't like this. I don't know whether it's the coronavirus, but you've been symptomatic since the quad's birthday party. Headache. Fever. Chills. I'm putting a cold compress on you, and I recommended antibiotics. Who knows for sure? Did you get a flu shot?"

Eve nodded.

Dawn wasn't smiling. "I'm going to test you now. It's not pleasant. Buck up, buttercup." She inserted a long cotton swab up Eve's nose, got her sample, and placed it in its sealed packet. "All righty then. It'll be a while before I get results. We have to assume you're infected. Rest. I'll check in on you shortly. I'm going to test our father, as he, too, has been having breathing issues. You may get really hot, but try to stay covered so you can sweat out as much as possible. Hydrate."

Beau assembled his things and blew Eve a kiss. He was obviously reluctant to leave. "How will she get food if I'm gone?"

"That's my problem, not yours. Get your gear and get out."

Beau grumbled as he walked outside. *Geesh, Dawn acts like I gave her cooties. Bossy bitch. I'm scared shitless. The death toll's rising. Dear God, what if Eve…*

Outside, the trees had budded, and some trillium was blooming nearby. Spring had come to the mountains, but Beau really didn't tune into the beauty around him. Instead, he focused on the sick *beauty* within the cabin. Worry coiled within his belly. *If this were a fairytale, I could kiss her and make her well or go on a quick quest for a magical cure, but this is no fairytale.* Still, he prayed for a happily ever after ending.

Dawn emerged from the cabin, as matter-of-fact as always. "This doesn't look good." She removed her gloves and placed them into a zip baggie. Then donned a clean pair. "Come here," she ordered.

Beau stepped forward.

She held the thermometer to his forehead. "Ninety-eight point six. Good. I don't think we need to test you right now."

He decided not to tempt fate. "Where do you want me to, uh, whaddya call it, quarter?"

"Stay away from folks, and I'll send a private to tell you where to go."

Beau bet he knew just where Dawn wanted to tell him to go—straight to hell.

Beau cleared his throat. "What do you think? COVID-19?"

Dawn looked at him. "What I do know for sure is this. It's not that her ruby slippers are too tight."

Beau bit back a chuckle. *They sure are twins, all right.* "What does she need? If it's blood…"

"I don't think she needs blood. We're set up as a field hospital now, but it's too soon to say she needs hospitalization. We're assembling more test kits. As soon as I have enough, I'll test everyone here. I'm concerned about John Weathers, too."

"I'd do anything for Eve. And her family, of course."

Dawn threw him a hard look. "I've heard that before, and so has Eve. When the time comes, we'll see, won't we? I know you don't want to lead her on."

Beau was taken aback. "She told you about that?"

Dawn nodded. "We're sisters. Twins."

"Yeah, I noticed. I don't remember hearing she had a twin."

Dawn smiled. "Speed dating doesn't leave much time for that, does it? Have *you* told *her* everything?"

Beau looked away.

"I didn't think so. Just the basics. Don't get serious."

Dawn walked back to the Lodge, intent on who knew what. But if he had to guess, it had to do with her sister.

Tell her everything? Hardly. I didn't tell her about Kyle or much about Jake. Kyle, who had been born under a lucky star until he wasn't. Until his cardiac arrest during basketball practice. Neither of us was even there. It was just an ordinary practice. Still, the guilt ate away at him. At Jake. At Deborah. *No, I didn't tell Eve much at all.*

The Jump Over the Moon cabin was across the semi-circle of cabins that curved behind the Lodge. Beau noticed a curtain part at the window. Deborah was obviously watching. *She probably thinks there's trouble in paradise.*

The curtains fell back into place, and Jake came outside to join him—standing the mandatory six feet apart. "Wassup?"

Beau stood there with his duffle bags and shaving gear at his feet. In a rueful tone, he said, "Covid-cuffing has come to a dead end. Eve has a fever."

Jake took a noticeable step backward. "Yowser. That's not good. Why are you standing out here like a motherless child?"

Beau forced a half-grin. "Someone's gonna tell me where I bunk next. Eve's quarantined."

Jake swallowed hard, and his voice shook when he tried to speak. "For real?"

Beau nodded.

"You could share our cabin. Mom would love that."

"The only one who might like that is you. Don't you remember the incessant arguing?"

Jake shrugged. "That's because you were always gone. You'd be here twenty-four seven."

Beau groaned. "Heaven, have mercy."

A uniformed young woman strode up to Beau. "Follow me, please."

"Catch ya later, Jake. Maybe we can go fish out back. You have to be a ways apart to do that. We'd be in compliance with social distancing. Ranger Luke Scraper checks the premises out daily. I'll ask him."

The private led Beau down the driveway and into the Elkmont Campground. She pointed at a military tent.

Beau gaped in surprise. "A tent? I'm bunking in a tent?"

The young private nodded.

Inside he noticed a lantern, a cot with a sleeping bag, and—if he wasn't mistaken—a Hudson Bay blanket. The tent contained a small table, a folding chair, and a campstool. A prong of the river ran alongside the tent.

"This is close to the restroom and showers. And as near to the cabins as I can place you. You'll notice you have towels on your cot." The private droned. "You'll continue to get your meals delivered. We'd like you to stay away from others for fourteen days. If you maintain social distancing, you can go outside, providing you wear a mask. You can use the charging station at the Lodge." She handed him a pair of gloves.

"Wear these when inside the Lodge. Here's hand sanitizer. Use it, and avoid touching your face."

"Yes, ma'am," he drawled. "Thank you. Am I free to fish and hike? I'll go stir crazy in this tent."

She nodded. "Just practice social distancing. Wear a mask. Wash your hands every chance you get. Take hand sanitizer."

"I know. You just said that."

She looked at him. "It bears repeating. Some people test the limits. Don't be one of them."

As he was settling in, Luke Scraper joined him. He, too, wore a mask and gloves. "How ya doin'?"

"About as well as you'd expect. Hey, I hear you fly fish?"

Luke laughed. "Not as well as Storme and Craig Knight, but that's another story. I do."

"Do you think you could teach Jake and me?"

"Sure. I go off duty in a couple hours. Tell Jake to wear a mask, and we'll get it done. I'll bring the rods, flies, and gear."

Beau sat outside his tent, savoring the sound of the stream. It almost sounded like a downpour on a rainy day. It was fast, furious, and loud. It should be a great sound to fall asleep to. *The snowmelt must be why it's so loud. That's a lot of water rushing past.*

While he sat there, he recalled the night he and Jake and Eve had watched classic movies together.

Eve made popcorn and brownies as they laughed and chitchatted. When the old-fashioned love scenes came on, Jake snickered.

"For real? That's how they got it on? Dahling?" He gestured dramatically.

He teased them about the endearments honey, sugar, and dear, and howled over the twin beds depicted on screen. "That's harassment, ya know. Dems fightin' words. Apparently, they didn't know anything about the future, being female."

Jake had them rolling with laughter. Eve threw a piece of popcorn at him, and a food fight ensued. They must have been loud, because soon after, Jake's phone pinged, and it was clear the caller was Deborah. She wanted Jake home. Now.

Clearly pissed off, Jake slammed out of the cabin. Eve and Beau pressed pause on the DVR to clean up. Now a team, they decided to wait for Jake to watch the rest of the film. Instead, they worked on the puzzle.

"Phew!" Eve said. "That took my mind off my headache, but I still feel whacked."

Beau looked at her. "A headache, eh? Is that a hint? No lovemaking tonight?"

"No, it's the simple truth. Ya know what? You're pretty easy to take on a twenty-four-hour basis. I feel like I've known you forever, yet I don't know much more than what I've seen and felt."

He grinned. "I know. Someday we'll talk more, but when we rip the scabs off, be prepared for bleeding."

"I think I can handle it."

"We'll see."

He tucked her into bed and kissed her on the head. "Sweet dreams."

He remembered going to his room, where he tossed and turned, worried in part and more than a little bit horny. *Like a magnet, she draws me. It's as if she has cast a spell on me. I can't explain the fast, mutual attraction. Like we're kindred souls. She's dynamite.* Beau prayed she did not have the coronavirus.

He sighed and stopped his daydreaming about Covid-cuffing with Eve, and the hot, pleasant moments they've been having ever since. *That was nice, but no time like the present to hook up with Jake.*

Beau enjoyed spending time with his kid, too. In truth, he had always loved being a father. His boys were the best things that ever happened to him. He texted Luke and waited for his reply. *What the hell. We can fish with or without Luke.* He had noticed fishing gear at the Lodge. *Mm, don't really need Luke...*

After that, he sent a text to Jake.

Want 2 fish?

His phone pinged, signaling a message.

Jake had replied with a thumbs-up emoji.

Beau had time to kill until Luke could meet them. He looked around and found a piece of white birch. He did a YouTube search, found what he needed about carving, and watched it on his phone. He remembered how to strip the wood using his Boy Scout knife, and he reviewed some other basic knife moves. He learned how to use the *peeling potato* and *violin* cutting techniques.

He placed the newly stripped wood on the table in his tent and practiced some other cuts he'd learned. There was something he wanted to carve for Eve. It was hard to get that sexy woman out of his head. Now she was hot, but unfortunately for a much worse reason. He spent his time occupied with whittling while he waited for Luke and Jake.

The two arrived at the same time, both wearing their personal protection garb.

In addition to the fishing rods, Luke carried waders. "You'll need these."

Grinning, Jake and Beau put them on.

Luke demonstrated how to hold the rod, the line, and use the reel. He cast several times to show how it's done. "It's *not* in the wrist. Use the forearm to thrust. Listen for the snap. Make an abrupt stop. Like so." he said. "Now, stand two llamas apart and—"

Jake laughed. "Why llamas? I'd say two bears apart."

Luke looked up. "Yeah. No way could you know. The LeConte Lodge at the top of Mt. LeConte transports food and supplies using llamas."

"Seriously? No way!"

"Llamas are surefooted and have less impact on the environment. They're perfect for the terrain. They're also big enough to use as a social distancing metric."

"Rad. I read online that llamas have some sort of genetic code or something that may help with the coronavirus."

Luke was impressed. "Those animals are sumthin' else. I wouldn't be surprised."

They practiced casting for an hour or so before the alarm chimed on Luke's cell, and he had to leave. "Quad Squad duty. Time to go. Enjoy." Then he headed for Amazing Grace and his family.

When Beau cast his line, he managed to snag twigs, bushes, himself, and a rhododendron bush, but no trout. Rarely did his line land in the water. Once, he caught himself on his jacket.

Jake laughed, looking as if he had been fly fishing all his life, and managed to catch and release two good-sized brown trout. "Finally! I found a sport I excel in."

"Good goin'. You sure do look like you were born with a rod in your hand. You were also born with a guitar in hand. I heard you jammin' the other night. It was Led Zeppelin, no?"

"I'm no Jimmy Page... Mom said I was making too much racket. She thinks playing my guitar is a waste."

Beau smiled at him. "I always knew you'd be good at it. That's all you wanted for Christmas. You take music and art seriously. Your knack for technology could become a career. You're good at that, too."

Jake shifted his weight and nearly slipped on a mossy rock in the river. He muttered, "Well, I'm no good at basketball, that's for sure." He grimaced, then grinned. "Or balancing, apparently."

"You know I was always worried about Kyle," Beau said. "What would he do for a living in the real non-sports world? The chances of a basketball career . . . Slim at best, and he wasn't the best. You, though, you have more options."

Jake grunted. "You mean I'm a nerd. Not a jock."

"I never thought of either of you in those terms."

"I did."

"Then you should stop. You're you. A gift. One that keeps on giving."

"Yeah. I give Mom a headache."

"Better you than me." Beau joined him in a laugh.

"I should have been able to save him," Jake mumbled. "I was there to pick him up after practice. I was early, so I went to watch him play, but he collapsed. I think he grabbed his chest, but I'm not really sure. He just didn't respond to CPR..."

"No one could save him. They used that school defibrillator, remember? It was too late. He died as he fell."

"I forgot about the defib..."

"That's why I'm the dad. I know things." He playfully punched Jake.

Jake seemed to brighten at the reminder that they had used the defibrillator.

They fished until sunset. Jake walked back to his cabin, and Beau hunkered down to whittle by the stream and think of his sleeping beauty. He noticed some dogwood blossoms had fallen like snow nearby. He picked them up. When the private delivered his dinner, he saw she had some for the rest of the semi-guests. When asked, the private pointed out the one set aside for Eve, and Beau added the blossoms, hoping to cheer her. He scrawled a note. *Is this a love note? Geesh.* He signed it with a big, bold B.

Thunder boomed in the distance, and rain began to fall. He ducked into his tent. *Home sweet home, be it ever so humble.*

After he ate, there was nothing to do, so he tried to sleep, not only to the sound of the stream but also the rain. He slept fitfully as the downpour from the swift and sudden spring storm split the sky. Lightning flashed. Thunder cracked.

Not able to sleep, Beau lit his lantern and looked outside. He learned why the locals called the stream a *prong* of the river. The stream was now a roaring rapid, no doubt the result of the snowmelt and spring rain. The water began to spill over, threatening to wash him and his tent away. Even as he watched, he saw his shaving kit fall only to be swept away. He had no choice. He had to evacuate. *And go where? Higher ground.* He pulled on his waders left behind from fishing, gathered his boots, and pushed whatever he could find into his duffle bag. He then made a beeline to the nearest cabin, Jump Over the Moon.

Chapter Nineteen: Lean on Me

I can't believe this. How can I be sick? I've hardly been anywhere… Then with a start, Eve remembered she had attended that Senior Speed Dating thing not all that long ago. She had been in contact with people from all over the country. The Great Smoky Mountains drew from the Midwest and the South.

She groaned. She felt terrible. Like she was drowning. Even worse than that. She felt like a used piece of toilet paper. She was hot and cold, literally at the same moment. She coughed a great deal. For the tenth time in as many minutes, she pulled on a thick sweater and soon removed it. As she did, she coughed, which soon became a heavy coughing fit. She heard a knock on the cabin door. She donned a facemask.

Marsha Weathers stood there with a jar labeled *Good for What Ails Ya* in her hands. It came in a purple bottle from Mellow Magic Apothecary. She also cradled a towel wrapped kettle of what was most likely soup.

Marsha gave her a wave and said, "This may help."

Skye had mentioned that her mother made the products she sold and that she had success with her lotions, potions, and syrups. Skye also told her the products contained cannabis. *What the hell. Why not try it?* Maybe she'd get a high from it, or most importantly, feel better.

"Get inside. You don't want to catch a chill." Marsha sounded like a mother hen. She even clucked. "John's been taken into isolation at the Lodge. I do worry about that old goat. If he up and dies on me, I'm gonna kill 'im."

Eve had to laugh because she already *had* a chill, and she

got a chuckle over the couple's banter. The laughing led to another coughing fit. She decided to take the spoonful of syrup Marsha pointed at her. *Down the hatch.* The concoction went down easily, and though her sense of taste was off, she knew there was whiskey in it.

Her body ached, and unfortunately, her innermost girlie part also ached...for Beau — despite how crummy she felt. She remembered the pleasant shivers he caused to steal down her spine. She could feel her skin burn from previously enjoyed kisses, and she swore just the memory of his touch was making her moist.

She must be hallucinating, because she felt his fiery touch that ignited her within and without. She could drown in the wetness of his kiss, the sensation of his hot skin against hers. She yearned to enfold him within her deepest parts and use her innermost muscles to squeeze his elixir from his hot, hard, pulsing cock. *How can I be so sick* and *so horny now? Was it Marsha's concoction? My fevered brain? Desire? That is some powerfully sensual tonic.*

She tried to eat the soup Marsha had left behind. It was unlike any she'd ever had, maybe. *Must be broth of some sort.* Perhaps it was bone soup? Or Fennel soup? Who knew?

She made her way back to her bed and collapsed. She hoped to sleep. She took a husband's arms bedrest pillow and used it to prop herself up, hoping to ease the tightness in her chest, and hopefully, breathe more easily. Eve ticked off her symptoms on her fingers. *Cough. Fever. Body ache. Headache. Loss of smell. Diminished taste.* Could it be the coronavirus? The odds said it was.

She wondered about her father. She thought of him as *John,* but he was the main reason for her visit. Oh, she had Dawn and her mom, but she never felt like she had a true or *real* family. She and Dawn had practically raised themselves. There were no grandparents, aunts, uncles, or brothers in her life — no family Thanksgivings. She wanted that. She and Stuart, her fiancé, had planned to make a family for themselves.

Stuart. Sweet Stu. Gone way too soon in another senseless, and in her humble opinion, unnecessary war. She thought preserving freedom was important and all, but going across the sea to the Middle East seemed so farfetched. But that wasn't how Stu had felt.

His had been a true and real calling to serve. He gave the ultimate sacrifice, his all…his life. Eve had never questioned his calling and had given him nothing but support, love, and encouragement. She had been ready to become a military wife — maybe make a family of a sort among the other wives on the military base.

Stu had been due home for Valentine's Day. They had planned to wed then, but a roadside IED had ended those dreams.

Now, decades later, she had found her bio-Dad, hoping to maybe kinda borrow his family… She was on the road to doing that.

She could smile now at the way they had first met. She had been at the Lodge, talking to Storme when he walked in with Marsha. When he saw her, nearly identical to his trio of daughters, he nearly — close to, literally — had a heart attack. And now he was under another kind of attack. This time it looked like coronavirus. Like her, he was in isolation.

She dismissed that thought and reviewed her introduction to the wacky Weathers family. What a trip!

When Eve had heard Skye needed help running the place, she'd jumped at the chance to get to know her half-sisters and her father. She'd pitched in and learned to operate the Lodge.

What had life been like with him? Storme suggested it wasn't all she had cracked it up to be. Eve learned John and Marsha had divorced, then remarried. Still, from her viewpoint, the family seemed close.

Mariah Windsong, her mother, never settled with anyone for very long. They'd led a nomadic life, moving from one temporary situation to another, never staying long enough for ties or roots to be developed. Mariah didn't even stay in the communes they found very long. Those stays were the highlights of Eve's life. There, everyone was family, but just as Eve would start to feel at home, for no reason apparent to her, they'd up and leave.

Over time, Eve had almost given up hope of ever having or creating a family of her own. Then she met a woman who called herself Whisper, who had taught her about God, His Son, and His Spirit. She liked the idea of a spirit family. Along with her sister, she learned about Mary, Joseph, and Jesus.

Eve had come to Gatlinburg to get to know John Weathers. Now he was also suffering from the same symptoms she presented. Only he was nineteen years older than her and a prime target of the coronavirus. Would she ever get the chance to be close to her father?

And then there was Beau and her growing, hard-to-ignore feelings for him. And his ready-made-family, Jake, now nearly grown. Another chance to find a family? She yearned to be part of a family. To belong with someone.

Before she settled against the husband's cushion, she filled a mug with more soup and drank some, keeping the rest on a nearby bed table. She closed her eyes to sleep, to dream.

Oh, what's he doing now? His touch is exquisite. Feather-light and perfectly placed stroking my skin. Making it so hot, I think I'll combust. I feel his fingers inserting, trying to go deep inside me. I squirm to try to embed them within me. But what I really want — his warm, hard, throbbing cock — he withholds as he fiddles with my needy nub. Is that his tongue? Oh my God! It is. He swirls his soft tongue around and around my dripping kitty. I scream out. My inner muscles clench and release. Oh, how I want him inside. Now, I silently plead…now. Come in.

Her own screams awoke her as she climaxed. It was heart-stopping and fierce. She reached for him…he wasn't there. Either she'd hallucinated, or he'd miraculously appeared and disappeared. She could be seriously horny, or she could be sick. A wracking cough seized her, and she found it hard to breathe. The bedclothes were a tangled mess. As she struggled to get up to use the bathroom, she tripped over them. The day had passed. How had evening come so soon?

Eve heard footsteps.

Dawn appeared.

Another hallucination? Why is she here? Wasn't she living in Nashville? Or was she back in California?

"Oh, my God, Eve. Look at you. What on earth are you trying to do?"

"Want to use…" she panted, "bathroom. Tripped."

Dawn placed a mask on her face and wiped her sweaty brow.

"You need help. I'll take you there. Lean on me."

After Eve relieved herself, Dawn helped her to the couch and covered her with a quilt. She placed a cool compress on her brow. Then she went into the bedroom, untangled the bedding, and remade the bed.

When she was done, she returned to the living room. "I'm leaving a radio with you — just in case." She demonstrated its use. "I'm also going to assign someone to check on you, take your temp and such. I have some chicken noodle soup from Millie, and Beau covered your tray with dogwood blossoms. That's all he could find that's legal to pick."

"Where is he?" Eve croaked.

"I've got him a nice cozy military tent caddy-corner to Jake's cabin. He's as nearby as I can safely permit. I'm going to have someone check on you every two hours or so. They say to try to hold your breath for ten seconds, raising your arms. Try to do that. Move, too, if you can, but be careful."

Eve looked at her like she was crazy. As Dawn spoke, she held the thermometer to her forehead. "One hundred and two. You get much higher, and I'll have to think about hospitalization..."

Another cough grabbed Eve. "No!"

"Just get better, buttercup. Relax, you'll go to our field hospital here at the Lodge. John is already there. You can heal together."

CHAPTER TWENTY: FEVER

Eve felt really bad. Worse than she had ever felt in her whole life. She radioed Dawn, hating to do so. She croaked, "Mayday, Dawn. I'm bad." *It's like having a wet sponge in my chest, not lungs.*

"Hang on. I've got you." Dawn replied over the static of the radio.

It was only moments but felt like hours before a small team led by Dawn carried her on a stretcher. They threw a tarp over her to shield her from the rain. When she was outside, she saw Beau with his duffle bag pounding on Deborah's cabin door. Tears leaked from her eyes. She wasn't sure if it was because she saw Beau desperate to get inside Deborah's door or the pain her body was in, but in that moment, she came undone. *Why, Beau, why are you running to Deborah?*

She was transported across the gravel parking lot in front of the cabins, feeling the incline as they neared the Lodge. She expected to be loaded into an ambulance and transported to Mountain Heritage Hospital in Sevierville, but was relieved to find herself inside the Lodge instead. Banquet Room One had been converted into a makeshift hospital of all things.

A nurse immediately stripped and dressed her in a gown while others inserted an IV in her arm. Another person put a cannula into her nose. She prayed they had something, anything, to give her that would ease her pain. She felt hands traversing her body and voices talking over her. She thought she heard *stat* but couldn't swear to it. She knew one voice belonged to Dawn.

Eve mumbled she was drowning and clawed at her throat.

A medic assisted. "She's suffering from delirium, Lieutenant Winters. Our options are narrowing. I've got something for her fever. Let's pray it works."

Burning. I'm burning up. It's Beau's doing. Why is he stroking my body as if he had the right to? I'm mad at him. How dare he? After running to Deborah, of all people! But I'm so hot. His lips on my skin are scorching me, torturing me. It's a good feeling but tinged with a sense of sorrow somehow. He's coaxing my mouth with his tongue. I want to let him inside. And not just inside my mouth. He's a consuming flame, making me weak with want and need. Flames shoot from his fingers as they trace their way lower and lower. He parts my thighs. I want him. I feel his hot throbbing cock, and I yearn for the relief only his cum can provide. But he stops suddenly, and I just burn up. I am enflamed with passion unfulfilled. Yet it's bittersweet. I feel him beside me stroking my clit this time, and at last, at long last, I give up. I come.

Shit! What's going on? Is that Eve? Where are they taking her? How could she have gone downhill so fast? Nothing I can do now. Wait. I can pray. Please, Lord, please. Help Eve! What if… Please, don't let this be the last time she sees me. There's no way she can know I was flooded out in the middle of a deluge. She probably saw me and thinks I reconciled with Deborah. Beau pounded harder on the cabin door.

Jake opened it, his purple hair tousled and standing on end. "What are you doing here?"

"Let me in. I have nowhere else to go. I'm flooded out."

A goofy but hopeful grin covered Jake's face. "You gonna bunk with Mom?"

Beau let loose an expletive. "No. Not gonna happen." He shook the rain off and removed his shirt and waders, then placed them on a chair near the fireplace to dry.

"You can room with me, Dad, but you have to take the top

bunk."

Every free moment Dawn had, she read the latest research. The vaccine was twelve to eighteen months out. That wasn't the answer for her sister. Remdesivir and ribavirin, as well as other medicines, were in use. Some doctors recommended and used a cocktail of drugs, including steroids. To date, no one here had been given those. In a pinch now, she pleaded with the doctor to try a drug cocktail before they had to consider intubation. Many folks who become intubated often died. Some did heal on their own, but clearly, some patients had not.

Dawn looked at the chart they had started when Eve first arrived. They recorded temperature and created charts for everyone brought in, so they could track their progress. Eve's temp was now 104 and rising. Her test results indicated COVID-19.

Days ago, Dawn had called for a medical team as things developed. This had not caught her by surprise. Already, they had three people being treated. Two were military, one was John, and now Eve became the fourth. They were using every medical weapon in their arsenal. The medical staff kept in frequent contact with the CDC, Centers for Disease Control and Prevention, and DOH, Department of Health, as well as the governor. Everything that could be done was being done.

Dawn was on sick watch now that she had managed her team. She was confident her unit knew what to do and how to do it. No one else had displayed any symptoms or tested positive, which meant the quasi-quarantine, isolating, and social distancing appeared to be working. So far, Mountain Heritage Hospital was not overwhelmed, and for that, she was grateful.

Still, Eve labored to breathe.

Dawn had no other choice. Either she tried the experimental drug cocktail before it was too late, or they had to intubate. John had already been placed on a ventilator, which they thankfully had on-site now.

The cocktail consisted of administering three pills taken orally over several hours. They had opened the windows to allow air to circulate. Good ole fashioned fresh mountain air, modern drugs, and a miracle, and maybe, just maybe, Eve and John could make it.

She propped Eve up and gave her the drugs while she could still swallow. And before she got worse.

Dawn needed to learn everything she could, not only to help her military family but also her own flesh and blood. Especially since two of those were here under her care. She was thankful no one else in her unit, the Lodge, or the cabins had tested positive.

She prayed the quads were safe. Word was so far, so good, but as new information poured in daily, that could change in a heartbeat. She knew where her family was and knew they were staying home, staying safe.

Still, she said her rosary daily, something she had not done in years. How they'd ended up Catholic was anyone's guess, but somehow, somewhere, the basics were in place. *Must have been Whisper. I remember Whisper poured water over our foreheads, making some sort of movements and whispering words. She must have baptized us.*

Beau waded through the morass of clothes littering Jake's floor. He grumbled as he climbed to the top bunk, hitting his head on the low cabin ceiling. Although he was now warm and dry, he tossed and turned, thinking about Eve.

She was a furnace that heated his blood, his body, his soul. *She's hot enough to melt iron, and damn it to hell, I want her. What kind of man am I, wanting a woman who's so sick? I'd like to jack*

125

off, but I can hardly do so under the current circumstance. I must be a rutting pig to think about sex right now. But the sex they had wasn't just two horny people feeding their lust. It was more an expression of deep feelings. It was a joining—a true coming together in a way he never had before. There was more to it than simple sex. The thoughts he entertained weren't about a sick woman, but one with a great temperament, no showy airs about her. No pretense. And she was gorgeous to boot. Inside and out.

She laughed easily once she determined a person was worth her time. Beau loved that she didn't suffer fools and had high standards for herself and others. He envied her wit and sense of humor. He enjoyed the banter she exchanged with him and Jake.

Deborah had never had a food fight in her life. She raised two boys but hardly ever really saw them as anything more than proof of a perfect family, along with a big house and social standing. When the boys were infants, she'd hired nannies, then farmed them out to a prestigious preschool as soon as they were old enough. Had even tried to talk him into boarding school! He had drawn the line there and was glad he did. As it was, he hadn't had enough time with them, and now Kyle was gone. Silent tears rained from his eyes. *Kyle. My boy. Gone.*

He was reconnecting with Jake now, seeing him through Eve's eyes as well as his own. And what he saw was good. Maybe Eve could find a way to help Deborah see that Jake's attire was a cry for recognition and validation and grief. It wasn't too late, was it? To fix things with Jake? To develop a reasonable relationship with Deborah? To let his growing feelings for Eve take root and flourish? He couldn't lose her, too. Not when he had finally found her.

He hadn't been looking, and neither had Eve. But apparently, fate, destiny, and God had been waiting for them to meet. He prayed he got the chance to make a better life with all of them. Maybe Deborah had turned to the things money could buy because he had failed her by working so hard, so long, so often. But by God, he could—no, he *would* do better from this moment on.

Chapter Twenty-one: Like a Bridge Over Troubled Water

Deborah woke the next morning to a familiar sight—clothes strewn all over the place. *Teenagers. Can't live with 'em, can't shoot them.* When she looked closer, she was amazed to find four waterproof boots, not two. *What?* Going over to the fireplace, she noticed the clothes weren't Jake's. Bemused, she went to the room Jake occupied and heard a set of snores. Her hand flew to her heart. *Could it be? How on earth?* The top bunk was occupied, and a dark-haired head appeared to rest on the pillow.

She quivered. "Kyle?" She climbed the ladder. Hope in her heart. *Could it be?*

"Kyle!" she cried. "My son. You're okay. It was all a bad dream." The head raised, and her eyes widened. Her shock made her fall off the ladder and land on her butt. "What's going on here? You're not Kyle."

Beau sat up and jumped to the floor. "Are you all right?"

She nodded wordlessly.

He helped her to her feet and steered her out of the room, carefully closing the door behind him. He put a finger to his lips. "Shh, Jake'll hear you."

"That boy hears nothing. He can sleep through a tornado. Why are you shushing me? You're the one who looks like Kyle, not me. You nearly gave me a heart attack. What are you doing here? Your girlfriend sick of you?"

Beau scratched his chest and ambled to his clothes, then

put them on.

Deborah never liked anyone walking around undressed and was happy to see Beau remembered that.

"Eve's sick. I had to move into a tent. The storm last night caused a flood, and my tent was washed away. There was nowhere else to go. I want you to be quiet, so Jake doesn't think it's always about Kyle. He's beginning to open up. He thinks he doesn't count. That he can't be Kyle. He's grieving and trying to find out who he is without his twin."

Deborah sunk into a chair. "Oh. My. God. Poor baby. So he's not rebelling."

Beau shrugged. "Yeah, or at least I think, it's hard to tell. He's a teenager."

Deborah fingered with the pearls she always wore. "I think a boy his age needs his father around. Breaking up our family was a mistake. Maybe if ..."

Beau sighed. "Is there any coffee around?" He stopped himself. "No, you drink tea. What was I thinking?"

Deborah bristled. "So drinking tea is a crime now?"

Beau looked like he was choking on his words or biting his tongue.

Deborah waved her hand dismissively. "Of course there's coffee. Make some if you want. Be my guest."

Beau laughed. "Good one. Looks like I *am* your guest. I didn't intend this. Mother Nature had other ideas for me. I'll talk to Lieutenant Winters to see where else I can stay."

Deborah pooh-poohed the idea. "It's fine. I was unprepared. You know how I like things to be well-planned."

Beau nodded. "Life is messy, and with the pandemic, it's messier and upside down. I'll be more human once I get some java in my system. It's good to talk. Truce?" He held out his hand and shook hers.

Her hand jumped at the jolt she still felt. *Perhaps it's no too late...*

She smiled. "Truce."

Beau looked as if he were laying down a heavy burden. "I failed as a husband and father. I was so intent on making money to give you and the boys the house and things you needed that all I did was work. I realize that now."

Deborah sighed. She had waited a long time to hear those words and had doubted they'd ever be said. She felt the anger and resentment she carried for so long melt. "I wanted too much. I like the lifestyle. Social connections mean a great deal to me. I wanted my cake and to eat it too. Believe it or not, I missed you then, and even more now with Jake acting out."

"I missed a lot, and I regret it."

"Me too." Deborah didn't know what to make of Beau. *Are we friends? Are we starting over? Will that help Jake?* "I've needed to hear that for a long time. I knocked myself out trying to compete with your work, but no matter what you did, I wasn't happy either. I have seen how you look at Eve and how she looks back. We never had that. We're too different, then and now."

Beau looked surprised. "We can never go back, but we can go forward as better parents and better people."

She nodded.

A loud knock announced that breakfast was there. The tray held toast, scrambled eggs, and bacon. It must have been the scent of the bacon wafting through the cabin that brought Jake out into the living room.

He rubbed his eyes as if he had never seen his parents drinking coffee together. "Wassup?"

Beau spoke. "Breakfast."

"Dope." Jake snagged a piece of bacon and noticed the coffee. He gave her a look. "Seriously?"

Deborah smiled. "What? I drink coffee — rarely."

Jake looked from her to Beau, then shrugged. "Sick. Think fishing would be good today, Dad?"

Beau laughed. "Not after that deluge last night. I have had

enough of the water for a bit. Up for a jigsaw puzzle?"

Deborah liked the sound of that. The atmosphere was usually supercharged when Beau entered any area Deborah occupied, but the scene before her was strangely nice and quiet...even peaceful. *Was that my fault?*

After they ate, the men cleared the table. Deborah found a pretty floral puzzle and set the box on the table. In unison, the guys groaned.

"What?"

"Boooooring." Jake rifled through the other puzzles, found one, and brought it to the table. "Try this one."

Beau looked surprised. "That's the Ghost Stag! Eve and I actually saw it one night."

Jake picked up a card from the mantle. "Says here it means soulmate or sumthin' equally lame."

Deborah froze and felt the blood drain from her face.

Jake noticed. "Awkward."

Beau found a trout puzzle and offered it.

Deborah said, "I think I'll read. You two go ahead. Do whatever you want." Suddenly, she felt chilly. "Suit yourselves." She donned her cashmere sweater.

"I can put on a fire..." Beau offered.

Deborah opened her book. "Whatever."

Beau grew quiet. "Wanna whittle, Jake?"

The two went outside.

Deborah read for a bit but soon fell asleep.

Deborah dreamed of the sun shining over the pool but low in the sky in the lovely landscaped yard.

She lay in the shade of the cabana, sipping a Tropical Itch drink.
Beau was flipping burgers, and the boys were doing cannonballs and Lord only knew what else as they sent a huge splash across the expanse of the crystal blue water. Laughter and splashes filled the air. She smiled. She did love her family. She wished Beau were home

more often, but he was here now, and for once, they weren't embroiled in a heated argument. She stretched and turned over on her belly to watch the muscle of Beau's forearm bunch as he expertly flipped another burger. She noted he had grilled some steaks, too, and smiled her approval.

Kyle called, "Look, Ma, no hands!" He catapulted off the diving board in typical, reckless abandon. He was too close to Jake. He'd land on him.

"Kyle!" She screamed, "Watch out! Kyle..."

She awoke with her heart pounding and ran a shaking hand over her face.

Jake came in, yelling, "It's always about Kyle!"

Beau followed Jake through the door.

Deborah raised a hand to cover her heart and raced to Jake's side. "Oh my! Is that what you think? That I love him more than you? I was dreaming of *both* of you... Actually, of all of us. We were in the yard. Beau, you were barbequing steaks and burgers. The sun was out, and we were having a great time. As a *family*, Jake, a family. You were there. We all were. Kyle was going to jump right on top of you. I was worried about *you*, Jake. It's not always about Kyle. Don't you ever dream of us as a family? That's all it was. A dream."

Jake shook his head.

"I was having a great time watching you boys cut up. So handsome and strong. Well and happy. But Kyle was becoming reckless, and I was warning him to watch out for *you*."

Beau didn't say a word, but he nodded to Jake, indicating all she said was true for them both.

Deborah continued. "A whole family. Is that so terrible?"

"Nah... Like, I guess not... Like it's okay. Tell me that story about the potted plants."

Deborah gave her son a gentle smile. "We were shopping. Easter was around the corner. I had Kyle in a carrier on my back. Your Dad had you. He bent down to get an Easter Lily for Memaw, and I bent down to get one for Memaw Jobs. When we rose to a stand, both of you boys had flowers clutched in your fists, pots and all. Shortly after that, you both released them, and they crashed to the floor, making a huge mess. We had to pay for them."

The family laughed.

"Remember the cuckoo clock we bought for you?" Beau said. "You were thrilled when you saw your first one. Kyle, not so much. But you cried when we went to leave, so we had to buy it."

"But…" Deborah continued. "My favorite memory is when you were in buggies, and we walked past the baseball field. Every time you two heard the crack of the ball against the bat, you laughed so hard the buggies shook. The players stopped their practice and came to the fence to get a gander at you two… Those were the days."

"We're still a family, Mother."

"Yes, we are, but it's fractured. It's different, but we're family, and I'll always love you and your brother. You were a package deal. I see how you hurt, and I ache for you, too. I may not show it or know what to say, but had I lost the two of you, I'd die. I couldn't make it without you, Jake. Tattoos, piercings, purple hair…the whole bit."

"You like my tats, Mom?"

"Well, I didn't say that… But I can say I didn't do a good job then as a mother, but I can be better at it now. I'll make one hell of a grandmother, though."

They laughed.

"Sometimes, you just don't know what you've got until it's gone," Deborah murmured in a wistful tone.

"There's a song like that." Jake grabbed his guitar, and they sang *Paved Paradise*. As a family.

CHAPTER TWENTY-TWO: DON'T WORRY, BE HAPPY

Three days later, Eve—while not dancing in the rain—felt like she was crawling out of the woods. Her body wasn't burning up, and she wasn't as achy. *They must have given me more than a medical cocktail. I think they gave me some serious sedatives.* Every now and then, she caught flashes of Dawn's face hovering above her. Her sister must have been in and out a dozen times, monitoring her, taking her temperature, charting the results. Eve slept a great deal of the time, but she did feel better now. Still, it was an effort to sit up.

She was more aware of her surroundings and was happy to see that both she and John were placed by windows. She could smell the fresh mountain air through the open windows, and every now and then felt the warming spring breeze. *Cures what ails ya.*

Vaguely, she thought she felt Beau's searing glance on occasions, but that could have been a delusion. What wasn't a delusion was seeing Marsha's worried face looking in through the large, old fashion window.

It nearly broke Eve's heart when Marsha pressed her hand against the glass as if trying to touch John. She caught Eve's glance and gave her a small smile and a wave. Eve fell back to sleep soon after.

Eve awoke hours later and was surprised to feel half-way human again. While she wasn't ready to do a happy dance, she could feel her fever was breaking.

The sound of John's respirator was even and regular, breathing for him. He was pale and looked so weak.

Eve felt so helpless. She prayed for health and healing for them both.

By the afternoon, Dawn returned with her cell and held it up for Eve to see. Beau was face-timing her. She produced a small smile but wasn't up to much talking. He was going on and on about something, but she hardly heard. Then, exhausted, she motioned goodbye and slipped into sleep again, allowing her body to heal.

No dreams or hallucinations or delusions followed until she felt the afterglow making love with Beau provided. How, she didn't understand, but she'd felt it with certainty.

Beau was excited. He had talked to Eve! Well, he had *seen* Eve, and she looked better. Her curls were looking like a huge Afro, but he thought she looked cute. Better. Maybe there was hope.

Dawn told him her temp was going down, and she was definitely not coughing. She appeared weak and tired, but after so long, what else could she be.

Meanwhile, his relationship with Jake and Deborah was improving. But he missed Eve and worried about her constantly.

Jake tried to comfort him, and surprisingly, so did Deborah.

"She'll be okay, Dad. You'll see."

Deborah looked sympathetic, with true concern reflected in her eyes. "She's not the at-risk group."

"But she has it."

When Dawn saw him, she said, "Buck up, buttercup. She's

a tough cookie."

Still, he found himself crying after seeing Eve through the large low windows of the Lodge.

Each day there was a hint of summer in the air, allowing Beau to spend time with Jake beside the river prong. The water had settled somewhat, exposing an uneven series of rocks they could use to go from one side to a small island between the prongs of the river.

Deborah began to pick her way over, holding her full gauzy skirt in one hand, using the other to balance. When she slipped, and a foot went into the water, it was hard not to laugh.

Jake called out, "Soaker, Mom. Sick."

Deborah just laughed. In the past, she would never have been outside near the river. She was a city gal who enjoyed poolside living. But she was different now, somehow. The tension she used to wear like a shawl seemed lifted.

The weather was so nice, they often ate as a family at the picnic table outside the screened-in porch. They were falling into an easy rhythm of living, venturing outside more often as the days warmed. Puzzles, once done inside, now lay half completed on the puzzle board carried inside and out.

They occasionally watched TV together. They didn't watch the programs Beau and Jake had with Eve, but they started to identify with the characters on *Survivor*. When Jake casually mentioned Eve or John, Deborah didn't tense up.

Beau was grateful his family was getting along, but he knew down deep that Eve was the one he wanted. If Eve saw them now, she'd surely believe they had patched things up, which he'd have to correct. But his admission of guilt must have released something within Deborah. She no longer bristled and appeared to understand that he had moved on. As Deborah seemed to forgive him, he began to forgive himself.

One afternoon, returning from a *window visit* with Eve, he spied Jake. His shirt was tied around his waist, revealing his tattoos. As Beau drew closer, he saw one was directly over his son's heart. He recognized the yin-yang symbol, but as he moved closer, he saw a red K appeared on the yang, and a J was almost visible on the yin. He closed the space between them, traced the letters with his finger, and drew his son into his arms. They stood like that for a long time, crying.

At some point, Deborah joined them and embraced the two of them. They made a family, each entwined with the other as they grieved. Together. Something they had not done. Healing seemed to bathe them like sunshine.

With no fanfare, Eve was released from the hospital. Medical assistants and Dawn held onto a belt band used to help hold her up should she weaken. A private carried a walker with a seat in case she needed to rest. She looked down as she walked, each step careful and deliberate. When she looked up, she saw Jake, Deborah, and Beau wrapped arm in arm. Together. She swayed at the powerful image backlit by the sun and the shadows that made them one.

She gasped and nearly fell. The group around her surrounded her, and the commotion split the family apart.

Beau rushed to her side — Jake and Deborah stood aside for the moment. But the others got to her first. Eve looked at Beau and felt her heart break in her soul. She would not break up a family. She and Beau were not to be. It was as simple and as heart-wrenching as that. She accepted Dawn's help and entered Mr. McGregor's. *Mountain Magic cabin, indeed. Where's the magic when ya need it?*

Dawn turned on Beau with a look that could melt hardened, air-cooled lava.

"Forget him," Dawn ordered when she turned back. "Take care of you. He's a no count."

But Eve's heart said otherwise.

Beau.

Shit! Shit! Shit! Holy motherfuckin' rotten timing. No way on earth, and nothing I say or do will change what must be etched in Eve's head. It's not what you think, sweetheart. Beau's heart was screaming, but his goose was cooked. How could he repair the damage? Did she even want him to?

In the end, he went inside with his family and was very, very quiet. After they ate dinner, he stayed near the fireside, whittling. Maybe his hand could show what words couldn't.

He had carefully kept after this wood. He made small deft cuts and sanded the wood as he worked it. His carving reminded him of the golden calf from the old Bible story. When Moses returned from Mt. Sinai, a golden calf had somehow just popped out of the flames, so the Israelites had claimed. This was no false god, though. It was the repository of the love he carried in his heart. Hours after Deborah and Jake went to bed, he carved.

Beau had carried that white birch the entire time he was quarantined, lovingly working every inch of it. He fingered it when he wasn't carving it, pouring in himself and his love with each and every stroke.

For a while now, he'd nurtured an idea for the carving. He carefully made each stroke of the knife work toward his goal. He knew what he hoped it would be when it was finished, but he was a novice.

He called to mind what he knew from his Boy Scout days, imitated what he'd seen John Weathers do, and watched endless videos, working it until he could barely see. Only then did he return it to the soft fabric he used to protect it and slide it in his pocket. Then he climbed into bed exhausted. *I'm still scared shitless. Please be okay. Keep on keepin' on, Eve. Forgive me. It isn't like you think.*

Chapter Twenty-three: I Can't See Me Lovin' Anybody but You

Eve poured herself into bed. Totally exhausted from the virus, not to mention Beau's family, she fell into a deep sleep. Dawn was planning to take her temp throughout the night and mercifully, hopefully, would find Eve had not deteriorated. And her temp stayed in the normal range.

While Eve's body healed daily, her spirits dragged. She recalled Beau's touch. It melted her as surely as butter on hot bread. His caresses were magical and could send her to her outer limits in a heartbeat. One long, searing kiss had her dripping with need and desire, the look in his eyes so sincere and filled with love. She could feel it every time he looked at her. When he had caught her gaze outside, she was overwhelmed by his tenderness...by his love.

Her thoughts played ping-pong between splitting a family apart or creating one, tempting fate or sealing love. Was it love or lust? Could her feelings be both?

Eve's windows showed not only lovely trees but friendly, encouraging faces of family and friends.

Beau didn't make it any easier on her. He texted his love and concern.

She sent a pallid emoji in return.

Every day she found blossoms on her meal tray and small carvings at her door. Some looked like a deer with legs too short, or was it a dog with legs too long? Maybe it was a wiener deer or wiener dog. It was hard to say. They were hilari-ous.

The daily window-side visits by family and friends boosted her morale, much like Beau's carvings.

Jake showed her his attempts to carve. "This was supposed to be a bird. Now it's a bird egg. Dad made a dog. Here's my attempt at a dog." It looked like a turd. On another attempt, his creation resembled a rudimentary shark, not a brown trout.

As spring inched its way up the thermometer, Jake's ward-robe sported shorts with no shirt and revealed his dragon tat-too, which wound from his shoulder to twist down his back and leg. It was beautiful, and she told him so. The blues, reds, and greens looked good against his developing muscles.

"You like my body art?" he chuckled. His hair was grow-ing and he now sported a mustache and goatee, along with his purple-tipped ponytail. Hair salons had yet to open.

Even Beau had a Covid-beard, with curling locks of hair. His haircut had grown out causing its long locks to get into his eyes. He constantly swiped them aside with good humor, reminiscent of the sweet-natured boy he must have been.

When she saw him, she said, "I like what you've done to your look."

His eyes twinkled as he stroked his beard. "Now I can do that and appear wise."

"Oh, and here I thought it was because you had me in your life."

A gleam deepened in his eyes. "Do I now?"

She nodded and felt at peace.

Marsha had told her she had cleansed her cabin with sage and peppermint. Eve knew some weed had probably been burned in there as well. Marsha had said it was for therapeu-tic purposes and would release serotonin to boost her mood.

Later that afternoon, she heard pounding and cussing.

Then groans and more swearing.

She looked outside to find Beau had made her a birdfeeder! He filled it with a variety of seeds. A tube of thistle was also hanging beside her window. The next day she awoke to find a hummingbird feeder nearby. She laughed. She saw it all as him trying to please her.

One day Deborah, wearing a mask, stopped by. "I just wanted to wish you well."

Eve was shocked silent. She nodded tentatively and fingered her mask.

Deborah looked well-pulled together despite Covid-hair. Her platinum hair graced the line of her jaw. "This virus brought some good into my life."

Eve's small smile wavered. "Beau," she choked.

Deborah nodded. "Yes and...no. Our family reunited."

Eve's face fell, and she struggled to block the tears that gathered in her eyes.

Deborah must have noticed and hurried on. "It only took a pandemic for us to see what's important."

Go away. Just leave. Don't say any more. Your words are causing chaos in my belly.

But Deborah continued. "I've had an epiphany. I could be bitter, or I could be better. Jake helped me chose better. I promised him, and I'll do it. There's something magical and healing about this place. The fresh mountain air maybe?"

Wait. Jake? Not Beau?

Then Deborah said, "I understand that you saw the hurt little boy in Jake before we did. You saw the grief. I saw the rebellion. Thank you, Eve. Get well. Be happy." She gave a small wave and walked back to her cabin.

I better stop living in my head. It's beginning to look like a bad neighborhood. Maybe I need an epiphany, too. Time to focus on the here and now. Wait. What...there's a bear...what? A bear perched on top of my birdfeeder! My birdfeeder on a pole six feet in the air! She grabbed her cellphone, snapped a photo, and sent Storme,

Beau, and Jake the picture of her exotic *bird*.

Two days later, Beau visited her, carrying a book.
What in the world?
He pushed it through the open window. It was titled *National Audubon Society Field Guide to North American Birds, Revised Edition*. Beau also brought her a *Backyard Bird Record* so that she could list what she saw.

Eve laughed delightedly. "Thank you. I doubt that there's a bear in there. It'll be fun to know what else I'm looking at."

As she watched the feeder, she recorded tufted titmice, pine siskins, flickers, juncos, but no bear. Still, who knew bears would feed on birdseed? She wondered if that one time qualified as feeding the bears. This brought new meaning to *Don't feed the bears*.

The bear she'd seen had a prominent brown spot. When she'd sent the photo to Storme, she responded saying she was fairly certain it was a bear she and Craig had named *Monday*, making his rounds. That night the bird feeder came crashing down, and that was that. She caught the bear smacking its lips! Monday had obviously returned.

The days of her quarantine were close to an end. She had been tested again, and the presence of antigens appeared but no new infection. She had begun watching classic movies on Netflix, and Deborah, Jake, and Beau had as well. She and Beau would text each other throughout the movies.

One night, looking through her window, she noticed the light in Deborah's room went out. She knew Beau could talk more freely now. Bit by bit, she was letting Beau into her life again.

As she watched the movie, she *FaceTimed* him when she noted somethings never changed and was surprised at some of the steamy scenes. Movies from the nineteen-fifties didn't necessarily mean a more innocent genre.

Eve told Beau, "Wow! Things really heat up in these movies. Not so innocent times."

"I'll say. There's a lot in their eyes, and the dialog is ripe with double entendres. It serves the story well. Took really good acting to convey all that passion."

"I wonder if it still works?" Eve asked.

"What?"

"Smoldering, hot looks," she said, throwing him a seductive look.

"It works. Now, stop it."

"Stop what?" she retorted, "this?"

"I'm warning you..." he said.

"Whatcha gonna do about it, handsome?"

"Remember what they say about paybacks. You're getting better each day. Soon I'll exact my revenge." She was beginning to miss that connection. The days fell into a regular pattern of visits, reading, birding, and meals with plenty of time to rest and heal.

Finally, her second COVID test came back negative, and she was allowed more face-to-face contact. Beau rigged up a contraption that could be placed inside her window. It allowed her to play cards and board games to prevent boredom but provided safe, social distancing at the same time.

One day she played Scrabble with Jake for money instead of points to up the ante. He insisted *lol*, laughing out loud, *lmao*, laughing my ass off, *awk*, awkward, and KP, kitchen patrol, were legal words. She laughed and allowed it.

"That's five dollars," he cried. "You owe me five."

Not one to be in debt, she grabbed her gloves and wallet, wiped down a crisp five-dollar bill with a bleach wipe, and slipped it through the window. Just then, Ranger Luke Scraper passed.

"Officer," Jake called, "I just received laundered money

from Ms. Windsong."

Eve's laughter rang throughout the hills surrounding them.

Chapter Twenty-four: All Ya Need is Love

Eve sighed. John Weathers was still suffering. Dawn had consulted with the doctors from an alphabet of organizations. The CDC, WHO, NHI, HHS, and BRACA. Eve wouldn't have been surprised if Dawn brought in NCIS, even though it did not deal with the National Guard, did it? They all agreed convalescent plasma therapy was in order.

Dawn approached Eve. "You know all that testing on you we've done?"

Eve nodded.

"You have enough antigens that your plasma could help our father. You share his blood type, so this may work."

Eve listened intently. "Go on."

Dawn continued, sounding more daughter and sister than a second lieutenant now. "Our father doesn't look good. We're out of options, but if we try this and it pans out, giving him your antigens, maybe…"

"Stop. No worries. I'll do it. But isn't it risky?"

Dawn nodded. "Sometimes, the only option left is the scary one."

"Do it."

As soon as it was humanly possible after pulling many strings—including with the VA, Veterans Administration— they administered Eve's convalescent plasma to John via transfusion.

Eve crossed her fingers. Marsha and Dawn and everyone else did, too.

It was as if they had prescribed *go-juice*. By midafternoon, the change in John was startling. He woke up, and they removed the ventilator. He was breathing easily on his own by day's end.

Eve bowed her head and cried by his side as she hadn't allowed herself to do in years.

Two days later, using the walker and wearing a mask, Eve visited John. Dawn was right by her side.

"I'm doubly…blessed. You girls saved my llama," John said.

Eve grinned. What a clever way to avoid the word *ass*. *His joke proves he's coming back to us.*

"You gave us life, Dad," Eve said, tearing up.

Dawn picked up where Eve left off. "It was our turn to return the favor. Give you a second chance to live." She gave them a small salute and left.

Beau had apparently heard the good news and walked over to John's window. A smile crossed his face, and his eyes lit up at the sight of Eve. He chatted for a bit and left soon after.

"Tell me about that guy who's been hanging around you. Is he a good guy? Good enough for you? Worth you?" John had obviously shifted into parent mode.

"That's hard to say." To her horror, she burst into tears. She told him the short version of their long story, including Deborah and Jake.

"Sounds like the man loves you."

Eve shook her head. "Naw. I don't think so."

"Things better out there in the world?" he asked. "I'm the only one left here. Those soldiers walked outta here this morning."

She nodded. "Yeah, a lot better. Governor Lee is opening

146

things back up. The quarantine is lifted for the summer, at any rate. They're hoping there isn't a second wave. It's too soon to really know, though. If you ask me."

John peered at her and cocked his head. "Then Beau could have gone home to Sevierville, Knoxville, Ashville, any-where-ville."

Eve thought about that for a minute. "But he didn't, did he? He must have stayed—for me? How 'bout that!" She was knocked sideways into next week with that revelation. *I did have an epiphany, after all. Wow…* "Thanks, Dad."

"All I ever wanted to do was give my children a hug or a kick in the ass. Whatever's needed."

She giggled.

"Remember this, Eve, men can't connect the dots, and when they do, it's usually wrong." John winked. "Now, git out of here before I mash yer taters."

Eve laughed. She thought about her Dad and Beau on her walk back. *Maybe I can help Beau connect the dots correctly this time.*

Chapter Twenty-five: Wouldn't it be Nice?

It's clear both Eve and John are out of the woods. Things are much better between Deborah and me. Hell, she practically gave me her blessing to go after Eve. What am I waiting for? A sign? Beau picked up the carving he'd just finally completed and turned it over, examining every laborious detail of his work. The white wood glistened and sparkled in the sunlight.

Jake walked up and nudged him. "When are you going to give her that, Dad?"

Beau shrugged. "This ole thing? I dunno. She'll probably throw it at me. She thinks I'm back with your mother."

"What? No way. That'd be weird."

He sighed. Although his family was in a good place, he was definitely not *back* with Deborah.

"Go give it to her, Dad. Go bold or grow old. And sad. And lonely. I'm gonna be graduating soon, and all. You got to get a life, dude."

Beau laughed. He had already packed his things and made his goodbyes with his family. He'd do as Jake suggested — take his stuff and go see Eve and then head back to his condo in Sevierville. He teasingly told Jake to take a hike.

To hell with it. I'm going bold.

Eve didn't answer his knock, so he boldly opened the door and went inside.

She was startled to see him. "If you think you can waltz

back in here and Covid-habitate, buster, you have another think comin'."

"We need to talk. No more quarantine, that's lifted. No living together. Just listen to me for once."

Eve flounced over to the sofa and sank into it. "So talk."

"Deborah and I—"

"Oh, puh-leeze. I can see you've reconciled… That's the big thing you have to say?"

Eve wasn't going to make this easy on him, and that was fine.

"No. There's a lot to hear. First, I've made mistakes. I can see why you think I went back to Deborah. We found a way to coexist for all our sakes. No, I don't want to live together. I want to tell you about Kyle and his death."

"Who's Kyle?"

"Jake's twin brother. He dropped dead of cardiac arrest at basketball practice. I wasn't there. Neither was Deborah, but Jake was. He thinks he should have been able to save him. He was a Boy Scout, after all, and knows First Aid. But there was nothing anyone could do." Tears leaked from his eyes as he knelt in front of Eve. "At long last, I have my ducks in a row. I know I love and want you."

"At least you know where your ducks are. Mine are all over the place like my emotions."

"Your ducks are in a circle. You have Dawn, Mariah, John and Marsh, the Weathers girls, Jake, and me—even Deborah. That's all you need. A whole family to love you."

Eve dropped to her knees beside him, holding him as he cried.

"Life is too short. You almost died. Kyle did die. I want to marry you. Before you say *no, we haven't known each other long enough…*" He took a deep breath. "I know we didn't discuss Dawn or Kyle before, but that doesn't come up on a first *speed* date, does it? It'd be a guaranteed bid for pity. I don't need or want pity, Eve. I want your love. Marry me." He pulled the white carving from his pocket. "I've been working on this since we got here. I don't have a ring, but I have—"

She gasped. "A hand-carved Ghost Stag. We don't need rings, Beau. We have all we need." Love shone in her eyes.

He could see it, and his heart overflowed with joy.

"Yeah," he said with a shrug. "All it took was COVID, Kyle's death, quarantine, and a pandemic."

Eve laughed. "It also took a legend and mountain magic."

"Is that a *yes?*"

She smiled. "Yes. Let's marry here at Mountain Magic cabin and continue the legend. Mountain magic cures what ails ya."

There was all the time in the world to tell him about Stuart, her engagement, his death. But now wasn't the time. It was time to celebrate!

"Okeydokey." He lifted her to her feet and swung her around, like in the old movies they watched with Jake.

And just like that, Eve found the family she always wanted.

The End

You may also enjoy the following from [Company]:

Mountain Wed
Kathy Kalmar

Excerpt

It was a glorious fall. The weather was warm with cool nights, which brought out the scarlets, reds, and oranges of the sugar maples. Poplars were crowned with sunny yellow, and brown oak leaves provided a welcome contrast. An undulating, leafy network of hardwood trees echoed the colorful leaves everywhere to fashion an autumn ablaze with splendor and unparalleled beauty.

Fall was a peak season for tourists, and Marsha's favorite season. It provided a bountiful harvest of seeds and petals needed for her stock in trade. When she gathered the fruits of the season, she felt reconnected to Mother Earth, Gaia, as well as her Cherokee roots.

Operating her own apothecary connected her new-age spiritualism with her mountain heritage. It allowed her to spread healing, health, and mountain peace to its people. Her only wish was to find something to bring John peace.

The war had done a number on him. While healthy in body, his soul and mind were tormented in the aftermath of war, destruction, and death. The few times he talked about the nightmares, he told her the carnage plagued his dreams and robbed him of sleep. In a heartbeat, something or someone would trigger him, sending him into a fathomless hell. Anything could set off his descent. Once she'd sliced her finger while paring an apple, and John's white, terror-stricken face told her he was reliving something. His strong firm hands shook as he rinsed her finger and examined her thumb. His breath came in huge heaving gulps.

"I'm okay, John. It's fine . . ."

But it was clear John was not okay. He was shaking, and once he bandaged her, he left her alone for hours. Just took off. Like a banshee was after him. She tried to get him to talk about it when he returned, but he shut her out.

"I'm fine. Don't worry."

Marsha used the ground leaves of valerian mixed with cannabis to calm his spirits, and passionflower and chamomile, to ease his nightmares. She added this to any tea she served him from sweet tea to hot varieties. She applied compresses laced with valerian but to no avail. Frequently she burned sage in their bedroom to bring the peace he so needed. Thankfully the negative ions released by the pines and the soothing whispers of breezes through the evergreens helped. Still, sometimes she wished she had the perfect elixir to offer. Most of the time, John appeared to cope and lived his life carving with the other craftsmen, looking forward to the births of his twins. But when the demons roared, he was lost to her and his surroundings.

Marsha pushed her worries away and was often in a contemplative but merry state when John got home from his work at the family owned and operated Lodge. She reveled in her pregnancy and spent her spare time making baby clothes. She also created talcum powders to use for her babies, and other elixirs and teas to help Marion, her mother, as well.

John spent his time working at the Lodge or on the cabin, and Marsha continued making and selling her products from her apothecary. When she wasn't doing that, she spent time applying lotion to her mother's failing body. Trying to bolster it with the latest herbal remedies that Dr. Cyd — as she had begun to call her friend — suggested.

When Marsha broached the topic of a water or home birth, Dr. Cyd stopped her with a simple declarative statement. "You may have twins." Wisely, Marsha did not mention doulas or mountain mid-wives.

It wasn't long before the approach of their first Christmas together as man and wife. Their lovemaking was gentle. At first, he had treated her like she was made of crystal or fine china. As the babies grew, he began to feel more comfortable and became quite inventive as the infants enlarged her body.

He'd chased her around the house with mistletoe, and when he cornered her, he'd often led her to the bedroom. Decorating had become an everyday event until her pregnancy discomfort intruded.

Emma Jean swore she had never seen more mistletoe in her life. "You leave that poor girl alone, John."

Unfortunately, despite the cannabis, Marsha was acutely uncomfortable during the latter stages of her pregnancy. Her ankles had swollen, and morning sickness became morning, noon, and night sickness. "Pregnancy isn't all it's cracked up to be."

Emma Jean and Marion agreed.

"It ends with a bang," her mother counseled.

Marsha tried yoga, hoping the stretching would help ease her discomfort. She and John attended Lamaze training, which again offered no relief.

Emma Jean was beside herself with joy over the impending birth of grandchildren. The pregnancy seemed to help Marion, as well. Marsha laughed when she overheard the two of them discussing becoming memaws.

Marsha knew Emma Jean went through agony waiting and worrying about her son, knowing his internal battle was ongoing. The family often witnessed his shouts and cries, resulting from his horrific experiences in Vietnam. His helicopter had been shot down on the way to pick up some wounded. For a brief time, he and his friend, Charlie, had been held by the Viet Cong. The army had listed them as MIAs, missing in action. That he had served as a medic helped. He had been able to treat many of his buddies, who were also captive and often victims of impaling from bamboo spear booby traps.

One time, John told her about treating a private, a puny, war beaten kid. He said the only things holding the patient together were the bandages he applied. He knew, in his gut, that guy wouldn't make it back to the base, let alone home. John was quiet after that. Marsha put her arms around him to hold him, but he pulled away. With time, she realized he was trying to spare her.

"Let me comfort you, John."

John looked at her. In a grave tone, he said, "Won't do him no good. Ain't no comfort for a thing like this, a man like me."

He often said that the men hadn't been able to tell who was an enemy and who was not. Guerilla warfare had been in play, and the conventional training they had received was often insufficient. Add in the jungle, the heat, the snakes, and the insects, and it had been a literal hell on earth.

Finally, returning home to the Lodge had been John's first step toward real healing. The Lodge seemed to be a magical place made even more so when Marsha came back to it. Thank heaven for the Lodge and his parents.

The Lodge was originally a rustic inn built to house the lumber industry's workforce during its advance into the Great Smoky Mountains. The timber barons had depleted the East Coast timber and moved their operations southward to the Elkmont area. Fortunately, lumbering was a thing of the past now, and a nice hardy second growth of trees covered the once denuded hills once more.

After the lumber industry had logged its last load, Emma Jean's parents had reopened the inn as a lodge for travelers as far away as Georgia and as near as Knoxville.

When Emma Jean and her husband took over, they re-named the inn Sugarlands Lodge after the sugar maple trees growing profusely on the property. They also had expanded, making the delicious maple syrup they provided to the townsfolk. The locals simply dubbed it the Lodge. John helped to run the place when he could tear himself away from whittling and wood crafting. Any spare time John had was spent either in the woods looking for downed hardwoods or spent with Marsha.

She and John frequently visited their cabin as John worked to repair it. He was just adding some finishing touches, so it would be ready to move into soon.

They currently resided at the Annex, a separate section of the Lodge that housed several apartment-like suites. They had their privacy but were still connected to the Lodge.

Marsha spent a lot of her time reviewing the notes she had on pregnancy garnered from her years of study at Berea College and time spent with her grandmother. She also applied what had Cyd taught her, trying special herbs and tea blends to promote wellness. She meditated, burned sage incense, used essential oils and candles, plus played soothing music along with her favorite folk and rock tunes. She talked to her babies and read to them, believing they could hear inside the womb. She ate as healthy as she could, including veggies and fruits, whole grains, and nuts. This was difficult when morning sickness intervened. She had to carry a bucket around for the times she couldn't get to the bathroom in time. That's when she left nuts out of her diet.

The approach of their first Christmas was marked by their first Christmas tree. John made beautiful hand-carved wooden rattles for the babies and a double cedar cradle in which to place the newborns. His skill had grown in the years the army had him. He had told her he whittled away his time whenever he could while in Vietnam. He had sent his carved rosewood pieces home where he knew Emma Jean would display them with pride. Marsha knew he hoped they brought his ma comfort. Though he wasn't there, at least Emma Jean had been surrounded by things he had carved. Marsha was proud of the fact his work was now getting recognized. More than one souvenir shop carried his black bear and deer carvings.

OTHER BOOKS BY KATHY

ABOUT THE AUTHOR

Kathy Kalmar lives in Michigan with Larry, her husband of nearly four decades. Kathy Kalmar, born in Detroit, Michigan, lives with Larry, her husband of nearly four decades. Lately, she feels her life has recovered from the bad country song-like life because her Smoky Mountain Tops Round House is rebuilt from the 2016 Chimney Tops II Wildfire. Her Michigan residence is enlarged by four feet with the addition of their new furbaby, Valentina. She loves to read and write contemporary romance novels. Meanwhile she remains fond of hot tubbing, chocolate, and sipping wine, mai tais and moonshine whether at home, Waikiki, Cape Cod or Tennessee. Y'all come back, hear? Currently, she is writing her next book. Aloha and Mahalo.

Follow Kathy at KathyKalmar.com